The Haunted Life

ALSO BY JACK KEROUAC

The Duluoz Legend

Visions of Gerard
Doctor Sax
Maggie Cassidy
The Sea Is My Brother: The Lost Novel
Vanity of Duluoz
On the Road
Visions of Cody
The Subterraneans
Tristessa
Lonesome Traveler
Desolation Angels
The Dharma Bums
Book of Dreams
Big Sur
Satori in Paris

Poetry

Mexico City Blues
Scattered Poems
Pomes All Sizes
Heaven and Other Poems
Book of Blues
Book of Haikus
Book of Sketches

Other Work

The Town and the City

The Scripture of the Golden Eternity

Some of the Dharma

Old Angel Midnight

Good Blonde & Others

Pull My Daisy

Trip Trap (with Albert Saijo and Lew Welch)

Pic

The Portable Jack Kerouac

Selected Letters: 1940–1956

Selected Letters: 1957–1969

Atop an Underwood: Early Stories and Other Writings

Door Wide Open (with Joyce Johnson)

Orpheus Emerged

Departed Angels: The Lost Paintings

Windblown World: Journals 1947–1954

Beat Generation: A Play

On the Road: The Original Scroll

Wake Up: A Life of the Buddha

You're a Genius All the Time:
Belief and Technique for Modern Prose

And the Hippos Were Boiled in Their Tanks
(with William S. Burroughs)

JACK KEROUAC

The Haunted Life
And Other Writings

EDITED BY Todd Tietchen

DA CAPO PRESS
A Member of the Perseus Books Group

Set in 11.5 point Dante MT Standard by The Perseus Books Group

Library of Congress Cataloging-in-Publication Data
Kerouac, Jack, 1922-1969.
 [Novella. Selections]
 The haunted life : and other writings / Jack Kerouac ; edited by Todd F. Tietchen.
    pages cm
 Includes bibliographical references.
 ISBN 978-0-306-82304-6 (hardback) — ISBN 978-0-306-82305-3 (e-book) 1. Short
stories, American. 2. College students—Fiction. I. Tietchen, Todd F. II. Title.

PS3521.E735A6 2014
813'.54—dc23
                                        2013039075
Published by Da Capo Press
A Member of the Perseus Books Group
www.dacapopress.com

Da Capo Press books are available at special discounts for bulk purchases in the
U.S. by corporations, institutions, and other organizations. For more information,
please contact the Special Markets Department at the Perseus Books Group, 2300
Chestnut Street, Suite 200, Philadelphia, PA 19103, or call (800) 810-4145, ext. 5000,
or e-mail special.markets@perseusbooks.com.

10 9 8 7 6 5 4 3 2 1

*This book remains dedicated
to the memory of its Lowellian muses,
Sebastian Sampas and Billy Chandler.*

Contents

Introduction: Jack Kerouac's Ghosts

"Jack and Edie lying across my bed,
Flying high like the spirits of the dead,
The living and the dead, the living and the dead.

Our Lady of Sorrows and the long dark night,
How many candles could I light
For the living and the dead, the living and the dead?

What's that black smoke rising, Jack, is the world on fire?"

—JOLIE HOLLAND, "MEXICO CITY"

Nineteen forty-four was a troubled and momentous year for Jack Kerouac. In March, his close friend and literary confidant Sebastian Sampas lost his life on the Anzio beachhead while serving as a US Army medic. That spring—still reeling with grief over Sebastian—Kerouac solidified his friendships with William Burroughs, Allen Ginsberg, and Lucien Carr, making up for the loss of Sampas by immersing himself in New York's blossoming mid-century bohemia. That August, however, things took a sinister turn: Carr stabbed his longtime acquaintance David Kammerer to death in Riverside Park, claiming afterward that he had been defending his manhood against Kammerer's persistent and unwanted sexual advances. Because he had aided Carr in disposing of the murder weapon and Kammerer's eyeglasses, Kerouac was charged as an accessory after the fact. Consequently, Kerouac was jailed in

August 1944; he married his first wife, Edie Parker, on the twenty-second of that month in order to secure the money he needed for his bail bond. Eventually, the authorities accepted Carr's account of the killing, trying him for manslaughter rather than murder, thus nullifying the charges against Kerouac.

Writing of these experiences in August 1945, Kerouac lamented not having "kept a diary of the events of the summer of 1944 [as] I should now have material for a fine book . . . love, murder, diabolical conversations, all." As it turns out, those events did find their way into book form—on more than one occasion—as Kammerer's death and Kerouac's initial immersion in Carr's social orbit were given fictional shape in *The Town and the City* and *Vanity of Duluoz*, as well as *And the Hippos Were Boiled in Their Tanks*, coauthored by Kerouac with Burroughs in 1945. Caught within the torrent of 1944, however, Kerouac did literally lose his grasp on a potential publication—though its subject matter had nothing to do with Carr or the tempting allure of bohemian life in New York. At some point late in that year—under circumstances that remain rather mysterious—the aspiring writer misplaced a novella-length manuscript titled *The Haunted Life*, a coming-of-age story set in Kerouac's hometown of Lowell, Massachusetts, featuring a character based on the recently departed Sampas. In *Vanity of Duluoz*, Kerouac briefly describes *The Haunted Life* as "the long novel I had been writing . . . in pencil," admitting that he lost the manuscript, possibly in a taxicab, and that he had "never heard from it again." Kerouac also makes mention of this mislaid manuscript in a 1954 inventory of his oeuvre, a handwritten list in which he boasts of having composed 1.5 million words, counting *The Haunted Life* as a "lost" contribution to that total.

The lost manuscript resurfaced, however, as an entry in the

Sotheby's auction catalog in June 2002. Fifty-eight years after its disappearance, *The Haunted Life* sold to an unnamed bidder for $95,600. The previous year, Kerouac's most celebrated manuscript, the *On the Road* scroll, had sold at auction to Jim Irsay for $2.43 million; that sale seems to have motivated the seller of *The Haunted Life* manuscript to test its value on the market. Evidently, the manuscript had been willed to the seller (also unnamed) by his longtime domestic partner, who claimed to have discovered it decades earlier in the closet of a Columbia University dorm room. Although vague on the details, this explanation makes a great deal of sense, as Kerouac had spent October 1944 living in Ginsberg's dorm room at Columbia after residing briefly with Edie in her hometown of Grosse Point, Michigan. While the thought of his manuscript making the rounds of Manhattan's streets in the backseat of a yellow cab probably struck Kerouac as both poignant and romantic, the truth of the matter seems to be that he had left the manuscript in Ginsberg's room after accepting a berth on the merchant vessel *Robert Treat Paine* (only to jump ship in Virginia and head back to New York). Why he subsequently lost track of the manuscript is impossible to say, though, true to its title, *The Haunted Life* eventually rematerialized in public sight like an apparition whose business in the world had been cut unexpectedly short.

In 1943, Kerouac had engaged in a less abortive stint as a merchant sailor, shipping out for Liverpool on the *George Weems*. Shortly after returning to New York, he drafted "The Odyssey of Peter Martin," a handwritten planning document for the novel he eventually lost. That document reflects Kerouac's hope that *The Haunted Life* would comprise a sociocultural history of the war era, seen through the experiences of Peter Martin, a character

Kerouac would later recast as one of the protagonists of *The Town and the City*. Kerouac began composing *The Haunted Life* during a brief sojourn in New Orleans in May 1944, and seems to have completed Part One ("Home") by the summer of that year. As Kerouac hinted in *Vanity of Duluoz*, the manuscript was written entirely in pencil on lined notebook paper (9 ½ by 5 ⅞ inches), and runs to a length of seventy-one pages. That total includes a concluding document, "Characters for Future Novels," whose placement suggests that Kerouac considered his drafting of Part One complete. This supposition is further supported by the fact that *The Haunted Life* is an autograph fair copy, meticulously written in the author's hand and absent of marginalia, corrective marks, and significant grammatical errors.

The cleanness of the holograph manuscript suggests previous drafting, though the relevant drafting documents appear to be no longer extant. As a result, much about the history of the manuscript and its composition remains unknowable, though we can glean certain information from the archival materials collected in the second section of the present volume. The absence of working drafts is compounded by the fact that Kerouac began writing the novel in a brief window between two of his most important histories of correspondence—one with Sampas and the other with Ginsberg—with the result being that no detailed record of *The Haunted Life*'s development exists in Kerouac's prodigious corpus of letters. Of course, some guesses can be made regarding the envisioned content of the novel's later sections based on the preparatory documents that remain, along with the plot trajectory of *The Town and the City*, in which Kerouac completed his rendering of Peter Martin in a decisive way. Those guesses, however, remain largely unreliable in the absence of a detailed plot outline or additional drafting documents, though we do know from Kerouac's documentation on the title page that he originally intended to write two additional parts (titled "War" and "Change"). This is all to say that although there is no getting around the fact that the novel lacks the ending its author originally imagined—in all honesty, we do not even know how unfinished it actually is—*The Haunted Life* nevertheless offers a telling glimpse into the creative life and imaginative capacities of Kerouac at a critical moment in his artistic development. Faced with this dearth of more detailed information, we should focus more intently on that which remains, as it does indeed function as a satisfying, if open-ended, narrative.

The modest, handwritten manuscript of *The Haunted Life* stands in stark contrast to the 120-foot-long scroll manuscript of *On the Road*. The scroll remains one of the most renowned typed manuscripts in American literary history, in which Kerouac fully explored what many consider to be his signature concerns, taking his place among a generation of postwar authors who infused American writing with transformative energy and verve. Although the early prose of *The Haunted Life* may lack the edgy charisma and experimental abandon of works such as *On the Road* and *Doctor Sax*, it nevertheless provides an important window into the intellect and intentions of the aspiring artist as he made his way toward the crafted prose of 1950's *The Town and the City*. That novel was Kerouac's *Dubliners*; like James Joyce, he began his authorial journey in the realm of realism and naturalism—leaving an impressive document in his wake. While it has become standard critical practice to dismiss *The Town and the City* as a derivative take on Thomas Wolfe, Kerouac's first published novel remains a compelling debut. Indeed, Kerouac arrives in *The*

Town and the City as a novelist already possessed of prodigious skills: there appears to be little the twenty-eight-year-old writer is incapable of doing within the confines of conventional novelistic prose. Deft descriptions of local scenery combine with convincing dialogue and an involving cast of characters to make *The Town and the City* a noteworthy novel of its time. It is now clear that Kerouac arrived so impressively in print partially on account of the writings collected herein, a selection of previously unpublished works in which we can hear the portents of the mature writer to come, while finding ourselves engaged by his lifelong literary concerns in their embryonic vestiges.

What also emerges from these writings is an image of the young Kerouac as a careful and thorough drafter of his ideas, committed to an artistic process that does much to refute the public perception of Kerouac as a spontaneous word-slinger whose authorial approach merely complemented his Dionysian approach to life. This recalcitrant image of Kerouac has been prone to damaging (and oftentimes lurid) exaggeration, and is ultimately more suited to hagiographic scholarship and accompanying forms of authorial celebrity worship than to a candid critical assessment of the intellectual range of his work. In turn, a more robust and balanced evaluation of Kerouac's merits might emerge from placing increased critical focus upon his reverence for process (a process that included generative writing, drafting, revision, and redrafting) and contextualizing his art within a richer set of influences and aspirations, both literary and historical. We might begin by being more mindful of the shaping influence of the 1930s and 1940s as first encountered in *The Haunted Life* documents, for (as we shall see) the cultural and social concerns of those decades cast a long (and ghostly) shadow over the remainder of Kerouac's work.

Kerouac set his fictional treatment of Peter Martin against the backdrop of the everyday: the comings and goings of the shopping district, the smoky atmospherics of the corner bar, the drowsy sound of a baseball game over the radio. Peter is heading into his sophomore year at Boston College, and while home for the summer in Galloway he struggles with the pressing issues of his day—the lingering effects of the previous decade's economic crisis and what appears to be the impending entrance of the United States into World War II. The other principle characters, Garabed Tourian and Dick Sheffield, are based respectively on Sebastian Sampas and fellow Lowell native Billy Chandler, both of whom had already perished in combat by the time Kerouac wrote *The Haunted Life* (providing some of the impetus for its title). Garabed is a leftist idealist and poet, possessing a pronounced tinge of the Byronic. Dick is a romantic adventurer whose wanderlust has him poised to leave Galloway for the wider world—with or without Peter. *The Haunted Life* also contains a revealing and controversial portrayal of Jack's father, Leo Kerouac, recast as Joe Martin. In contrast to Garabed and his progressive, New Deal perspective, Joe is a right-wing, bigoted populist and an ardent admirer of radio personality Father Charles Coughlin. The conflicts of the novel are primarily intellectual, then, as Peter finds himself suspended between the differing views of the other three characters regarding history, politics, and the world, and struggles to define what he believes to be true and worthy of his intellect and talents.

Kerouac modeled this form of dialogue-based intellectual

drama on the works of Fyodor Dostoevsky, a point he would explicitly stress in his planning documents for *The Town and the City*. Writing of his intentions for the eldest three Martin brothers in that novel, Kerouac explained that "these three brothers—Peter, Francis, and Joe—represent the three alternatives of adjustment to American life, as the Karamazov brothers were in Dostoevsky's Russia." *The Brothers Karamazov* is primarily a novel of ideas, in which the principal characters represent different philosophical positions; the same can be said of *The Possessed* (now usually titled *Demons* in English translations), another Dostoevsky novel of which Kerouac was particularly fond. Much of the conflict in these novels is generated from the clash and evolution of dissimilar philosophies as the narratives unfold, testing the validity or wisdom of each character's particular position. In Kerouac's *The Haunted Life*, Joe, Garabed, and Dick might also be said to represent "three alternatives of adjustment to American life" during the critical historical period stretching from the Great Depression to the outbreak of World War II. Rooted in the 1930s, these voices or perspectives emanate from one of the most raucous periods in American history and speak vividly of an era in which the nation came remarkably close to revolutionary rupture.

The young Kerouac was certainly caught up in the period's revolutionary vibe, as was the idealistic Sampas. Consider, for instance, the March 1943 letter to Sampas in which an exuberant Kerouac proposes traveling to Russia to lay a wreath on the socialist writer John Reed's grave. Earlier in that same letter, Kerouac proclaims, "AFTER THE WAR, WE MUST GO TO FRANCE AND SEE THAT THE REVOLUTION GOES WELL! AND GERMANY TOO! AND ITALY TOO! AND RUSSIA!" These revolutionary enthusiasms (expressed in full capitalization) might be attributed to what Michael Denning has identified as a pronounced "laboring" of American culture during the 1930s, in which the working classes and "common people" became the dominant subject matter of the nation's culture industries—just as they became the focus of the era's political rhetoric and the organizing efforts of the Congress of Industrial Organizations (CIO). This phenomenon was fostered in American letters by figures such as *New Masses* editor Mike Gold and groups such as the John Reed Clubs, and Kerouac's discussion in a 1942 notebook of what he calls "the trinity" of great American writers bears the vestiges of this laboring: although he includes Thomas Wolfe in his trinity, he also names William Saroyan and Albert Halper, both of whom might be convincingly identified with the cultural transformations described by Denning.

Kerouac's admiration for Wolfe, meanwhile, remains undeniable. The lyrical regionalism of Wolfe's *Look Homeward, Angel* (1929), which fictionalized the author's coming-of-age in Asheville, North Carolina, undoubtedly colored Kerouac's own account of his upbringing in Lowell. Indeed, the gushing exuberance of Wolfean prose can be seen quite vividly in the impressionistic portrayal of Galloway that appears near the end of *The Haunted Life*'s opening chapter (beginning with the phrase "Here in Galloway—"). However, this poetic description of small-town life emerges in stark contrast to the stripped-down, realist prose animating the text up until that point—a style more in keeping with the labor-focused realism of writers such as Saroyan and Halper. Saroyan's 1939 play, the Pulitzer Prize–winning *The Time of your Life*, vaulted the California writer to the heights of the nation's literary culture. Focused predominantly on the denizens of a San Francisco saloon, the play thoughtfully renders each character's hopes and aspirations for the future. In the bulk of his work, however, Saroyan gravitated toward the portrayal of Armenian American agricultural workers in California's San Joaquin Valley, especially in his hometown of Fresno. In the Fresno writings—of which the short-story collection *My Name is Aram* (1940) is particularly representative—Saroyan depicted agricultural workers and their families with a high degree of realism and grit, a quality that must have spoken to the young Kerouac, who always possessed an instinctive empathy for Lowell's working people and the communities they inhabited (though not necessarily for the mills in which they labored). In a sense, certain of Kerouac's later works, such as *Doctor Sax* and *Visions of Gerard,* attempt to replicate Saroyan's feat in relation to Lowell's Franco-American community. Kerouac's background in Lowell also goes a long way toward explaining his fascination with Albert Halper, whose reputation has seriously declined since the days when Kerouac included him in his trinity of influences. Halper was more pronouncedly involved in proletarian aesthetics than Saroyan, and in naturalistic works such as *The Foundry* (1934) he offered a convincing portrayal of Chicago factory workers that obviously struck a chord with Kerouac, reminding him of his experience growing up in a New England mill town.

In keeping with the "laboring" of culture discussed above, many American writers in the 1930s and early 1940s directed their creative attention toward the "common people," as much of the population struggled to survive the challenging economic circumstances of the time. On account of that artistic focus, Depression Era writing became newly imbued with the concerns of literary realism and naturalism, and these concerns are evident throughout *The Haunted Life*. Moreover, the political idealism driving the era's aesthetic transformations is manifested in the figure of Garabed, whose philosophy is clearly modeled after the leftist and humanist exuberance of Sebastian Sampas. In a sense, the political enthusiasms of Kerouac's youth died with Sampas at Anzio. Nevertheless, in works such as *The Haunted Life* and *The Town and the City,* we find Sampas encased in the amber of his unabashed ideals. The war in which Sebastian lost his life effectively ended the Depression, and the onset of the Cold War positioned the United States against the Soviet Union in a geopolitical contest for the world's hearts and minds (despite the nations' recent wartime alliance against fascism). These postwar developments tarnished socialist principles for many American thinkers—as did the critiques of Soviet totalitarianism contained in works such as Arthur Koestler's *Darkness at Noon* (1940) and George Orwell's *1984* (1948), both of which served as fictional precursors to Hannah Arendt's influential *The Origins of Totalitarianism* (1951). The looming specter of the Soviet Union and the terrifying uncertainties of the nuclear arms race made the class-based concerns of prewar literary works such as John Steinbeck's *Grapes of Wrath* and John Dos Passos's *U.S.A.* trilogy seem suddenly antiquated, and the reputation of proletarian writers such as Halper evaporated within the pressures of the new political climate. Furthermore, as Morris Dickstein has pointed out, the political agitator who featured so prominently in 1930s proletarian literature was replaced in the 1950s by "prickly nonconformists" such as Kerouac's Sal Paradise and J. D. Salinger's Holden Caulfield, whose actions are geared toward escape rather than revolutionary social transformation; Paradise and Caulfield seek out new forms of freedom and vitality on the margins of mainstream Cold War culture in ways that ultimately have very little to do with political doctrines on either end of the spectrum. As Dickstein goes on to explain, postwar rebellion located its nemesis in an American mindset suddenly "more devoted to organizational values and social conformity, more homogenous in its stated ideals," a phenomenon amply explored in several major sociological works of the period, including *The Lonely Crowd* (1950) and C. Wright Mills's *White Collar* (1951). It is quite possible that if Sampas had survived the war, he would have found his own views dramatically refashioned by these Cold War intellectual trends—as Kerouac and many others did. As things stand, however, Sampas inhabits Kerouac's work as an emblem of the leftist idealism and utopian aspirations that infused so many young lives in the years just prior to World War II.

As we've seen, in the decade leading up to that war, American political and artistic culture came to be animated by a pronounced rhetoric of the people. Some of this rhetoric was markedly leftist and utopian—as in the case of Kerouac's letter to Sampas—while some of it tended toward divisiveness and xenophobia, as in the case of Father Charles Coughlin, who garners an explicit reference in *The Haunted Life*. This reference appears in the midst of a conversation with Garabed regarding Joe Martin's bigoted worldview, in which Peter declares his father a "Coughlinite." As Alan Brinkley has observed, by the late 1930s Coughlin had become "one of the nation's most notorious extremists: an outspoken anti-Semite, a rabid anticommunist, a strident isolationist, and, increasingly, a cautious admirer of Benito Mussolini and Adolf Hitler." The New Deal, however, was the chief target of his vitriol, and he viewed the era's reforms as an aggressive expansion of industrialized bureaucracy, presided over by Franklin D. Roosevelt, whom Coughlin frequently dismissed as a "tyrant." This intense disdain for Roosevelt is evident in Joe Martin's worldview—as it is in Leo Kerouac's letters, collected in the third section of this volume. (In the letters, Leo refers to the president derisively as "Roosie" and to the first lady as "Eleanoah.")

Coughlin had entered the priesthood through the Basilian order, known for its devotion to Catholic forms of social activism. These forms had first taken hold amidst the industrial upheavals of nineteenth-century Europe and would prove in Coughlin's early oratory to appeal to large segments of the Depression Era working class, whose ranks had been greatly augmented by the rise in European Catholic immigration at the beginning of the twentieth century. Generally speaking, Roosevelt possessed sizable appeal among this working-class population; in fact, Coughlin originally entered public life as a supporter of Roosevelt, drawn to the president's critique of bankers and the moral shortcomings of modern capitalism. Coughlin's break with Roosevelt occurred in the mid-1930s over what he viewed as the tyrannical and communistic aspects of the Second New Deal—at which point he began to refer to the president regularly as a "dictator." By 1938, Coughlin's rhetoric had taken a detour into the ugliest precincts of populism and xenophobia, devolving ultimately into the overt anti-Semitism expressed in *The Haunted Life* by Joe Martin.

For Joe, like so many of his time, radio represents a lifeline to the larger world; not coincidentally, it was also Coughlin's preferred medium. He began delivering radio sermons in 1926, and at the peak of his popularity his listenership surpassed the 30 million mark. In a sense, Coughlin served as the forerunner of a postwar evangelical culture that found ways to disseminate its politicized brand of conservative Christianity through the newest and most popular media channels (and continues to do so today). In his own time—as Brinkley has documented—Coughlin's rhetoric proved extremely attractive to those portions of the population experiencing apprehension over what proved to be a significant renovation of the nation's life patterns and institutional structures. As Brinkley explains, "the United States in the 1930s was in the late stages of a great transformation already many decades old: a change from a largely rural, provincial, fragmented society to a highly urban, industrial one linked together by a network of large institutions." This transformation—as Charles and Mary Beard had foreseen in *The Rise of American Civilization* (1927)—was chiefly facilitated by radio and the automobile, both of which unified American culture to an unprecedented degree. Lingering islands of provincialism could delay their contact with the conditions of modern life no longer, and the tensions arising from this contact are a central theme of both *The Haunted Life* and *The Town and the City*.

In *The Haunted Life,* Kerouac frames these historical tensions within the family drama of the Martins. The narrative opens with Joe Martin engaged in an openly racist and xenophobic diatribe, as jarring as the invective of Pap in Mark Twain's *Adventures of Huckleberry Finn*. As Joe blows cigar smoke like a dragon and bemoans the collapse of his beloved country instigated by foreigners and people of color, Peter drifts toward the radio and turns up an unnamed recording by Benny Goodman. Peter's actions instantly transform the radio into a site of profound cultural conflict, as Goodman's music represents a signal from the modern world that Joe's provincialism can no longer ignore. In addition to being hailed as the "King of Swing," Goodman emerged as a hero of the 1930s American left on account of his contributions to racial causes. After hiring pianist Teddy Wilson as part of his trio in 1935, Goodman created the first racially integrated music recordings in American history. Moreover, Wilson himself was known as a tireless supporter of the left-wing causes so dear to Garabed (and Sampas), and had served as the featured performer at benefit concerts for *New Masses* magazine. Rounding out the Goodman trio was drummer Gene Krupa, himself the son of a Polish immigrant. Goodman's trio, in other words, provides a vivid sonic analogue of the cultural transformations lambasted by Joe—a fact Kerouac deftly reinforces as the elder Martin continues to curse Jewish and black Americans over the backdrop of Goodman's music.

In this brief opening episode, the novel effectively foreshadows its concerns with social, political, and cultural history, demonstrating that Kerouac was already developing a sound understanding of the elements of fiction. Indeed, the book ushers us immediately into the political divisions of the time, as Garabed's left-leaning optimism soon provides a counterweight to the right-wing vituperations of Joe. Over the course of what follows, however, Joe Martin's insular thinking is also countered in Peter's mind by the promise of flight, as represented by the wanderlust of Dick Sheffield. It is Dick, after all, who interrupts Peter's opening reverie (in Chapter Four) regarding the intrinsic decency of the American suburbs. Unlike the daydreaming Peter—who is enraptured at times by the pastoral elements of his hometown—Dick is always harboring a new plan of escape from what he views as a bucolic and undesirable existence in provincial Galloway. In the words of the narrator, Dick "never made himself too comfortable, he was always ready to resume his energies." Through the figure of Dick, then, Kerouac evokes the restive American spirit long embodied in the national iconography of the West—an iconography that has persistently wedded the promise of escape from ossified civilization (represented in this text by the reactionary rhetoric of Joe Martin) to fantasies of liberation and self-reliance. Moreover, Dick has a deep faith in the superiority of firsthand experience, a belief Kerouac himself (who always remained an urban transcendentalist of sorts) shared with the New England romantics who preceded him. At heart, Dick's romanticism seems quite at home within the early work of an author whose most renowned novel—*On the Road*—would unabashedly celebrate the expansion of American experiential capacities as enabled by automobile culture, while providing the perfect literary accompaniment to the passage of the Federal-Aid Highway Act of 1956.

The conflicting attitudes and concerns of *The Haunted Life*'s characters permeate much of Kerouac's work, reflecting the early influence of friends such as Sampas and Chandler. As prototypes, these figures provide the Kerouacian protagonist with two possible alternatives to the allure of domestic life and the hearth in midcentury America, one cerebral and one romantic. Moreover, while it is undeniable that Neal Cassady and Allen Ginsberg served as the respective inspirations for the neo-romantic Dean Moriarty and the poetic idealist Carlo Marx of *On the Road*, we might locate the embryonic vestiges of these character types in the fictional specters of Dick and Garabed. That is to say, while much has been made of the influence of New York bohemia on Kerouac's aesthetic evolution—and rightly so—early works such as *The Haunted Life* compel us to consider the extent to which many of the author's primary tropes and concerns originated in his upbringing in Lowell. The recent publication of *The Sea Is My Brother*, written in 1942 and unpublished during Kerouac's lifetime, provides further justification for such considerations, as the book's two male protagonists at one point embark on a road trip from New York to Boston (the geographical stretch of America most familiar to the twenty-year-old Kerouac), presaging the epic road journeys of his most famous work.

Sampas and Chandler remain spectrally preserved in the protracted act of memorialization that is Kerouac's *Duluoz Legend,* the title given by the author to his full output of semiautobiographical works. Evidently, however, the act of remembering never fully released him from bereavement, or from his personal hauntings. Thus, Kerouac's fiction wrestles with the fact that our ghosts often return, despite their ceremonial burials; we carry them, impressed upon our memory, across the arc of our own brief encounter with time, until we can no longer speak or write their names. Early in 1944, Kerouac composed another novella, *Galloway,* which he identified as a revised version of a 1942 work titled *The Vanity of Duluoz* (not to be confused with 1967's *Vanity of Duluoz*). In *Galloway,* Kerouac cast himself as Michael Daoulas and Sampas as Christopher Santos, and made some rudimentary attempts at stream of consciousness and at constructing multiple, concurrent narrative lines (an element of storytelling he would largely abandon following *The Town and the City*). As Joyce Johnson explains, Kerouac soon transposed the concerns of *Galloway* into the pages of *The Haunted Life*—though it should be pointed out that these two early works are drastically different novels at the level of voice and style, as *Galloway* attempts to mimic the high-modernist experimentation of writers such as William Faulkner, James Joyce, and Kerouac's beloved Marcel Proust, while *The Haunted Life* remains more clearly under the influence of Kerouac's "trinity." Perhaps the most striking moments in the *Galloway* draft occur on its final page, where we encounter a set of spontaneous reflections extraneous to the concerns of the narrative proper. A handwritten inscription in the upper right-hand margin of the concluding page suggests that *Galloway* was completed "while listening to Handel's 'Messiah,' Easter, 1944." At the bottom of that same page—separated from the concluding lines of the narrative by a string of asterisks—is a prayer of sorts, suggesting that Kerouac finished the piece while in mourning over the news of Sebastian Sampas's death (which had occurred on March 2). That section reads as follows:

> I wish to be devout, but not on my knees in the church of the Lord. Oh where can I be devout, and to what great power, and for what end? Here in the pine wood, where the arch is Gothic, and the light rays earthward, where the trunks are buttressed, and the sighing wind is an organ sound, to what end and wherefore devout? Oh Splendid watcher . . . my brother . . . supreme soul of the earth, are you with me now? Were I to pray, would you hear? Were I to sing, would you hear? Were I, yes, to weep, would you hear? Your form, your shadow I seek, and almost find, and then lose, and sense again.

Shortly after composing these lines, Kerouac would begin work on *The Haunted Life*. One of the epigraphs chosen for that work was an excerpt from Milton's pastoral elegy "Lycidas," making it abundantly clear that *The Haunted Life* was to serve as a literary requiem for Sampas and Chandler—and perhaps a host of others.

Chandler had lost his life earlier in the war on the Bataan Peninsula. Moreover, in February 1943, the *Dorchester*—on which Kerouac had previously shipped out as a merchant seaman—was sunk by a German submarine, an incident in which many of Kerouac's former shipmates lost their lives. Such losses made Kerouac particularly sensitive about the male relationships in his life, as they compounded a deeply rooted insecurity traceable to the death of his brother, Gerard, when Jack was only four years old. At several points in *The Town and the City*, Kerouac writes poignantly of male loneliness, observing that "men are always lonely" and that "each one of them burned and raged with a particular loneliness, a special desolate anger and longing." In such moments, he seems in part to be engaging with sentiments forged within the tenuous male bonds of the wartime years. Indeed, Kerouac's losses during those years go a long way toward explaining his particular fascination with male friendship or male bonding in virtually all of his books.

The impulse to record—to submit memory to print—is another of the animating features of those books. Throughout *The Duluoz Legend*, Kerouac goes to great lengths to detail the transformative events of his own life while simultaneously chronicling the lives of so many he met along the way. At its core, this compulsion seems driven by the author's keen awareness of the transience of existence, a lesson from the wartime years that Kerouac carried through the remainder of his days. While Kerouac discovered much of the inspiration for his prose style in the improvisatory nature of jazz, this longing to memorialize bears a notable resemblance to the artistic motivations of the Russian composer Dmitri Shostakovich. In reflecting on his own experiences of World War II, Shostakovich makes a startling admission:

> The majority of my symphonies are tombstones. Too many of our people died and were buried in places unknown to anyone, not even their relatives. It happened to many of my

friends. Where do you put the tombstone for Meyerhoff or Tukhachevsky? Only music can do that for them. I'm willing to write a composition for each of the victims, but that's impossible, and that's why I dedicate my music to them all. I think constantly of these people, and in almost every major work I try to remind others of them.

Particularly striking about Shostakovich's statement is his accompanying confession that the commemoration of those lost is ultimately "impossible." Nor have his symphonic efforts freed the composer from the burden of memory, as he acknowledges thinking "constantly" of those who have perished. Such disclosures rub powerfully against the grain of our conventional understanding of memorialization and monument building. That is to say, we have long supposed that the purpose of constructing monuments and memorials is to relegate individual or cultural loss respectfully to the past—an idea whose roots in Western consciousness might be traced to Pericles's Funeral Oration in Thucydides's *History of the Peloponnesian War*. Accordingly, acts of memorialization are to serve as mechanisms of dissociation even as they foreground commemoration—they are markers of the past that allow the living to move on.

Nevertheless, much of Kerouac's work continues to revolve around its originating sense of loss, as if the act of recalling or commemorating can never fully liberate him from the things being recalled. Like Shostakovich, Kerouac remains haunted and seems unable to resist the impulse to "remind others." This impulse is plainly evident in works such as 1967's *Vanity of Duluoz*, in which he circles back through many of the events that originally served as the basis of *The Town and the City*. This quality of

Kerouac's oeuvre makes it the improbable prose counterpart of Shostakovich's symphonic work—an epic literary cycle of memorialization—and the affinities between these two artists do not stop there. Like many intellectuals and artists who lived through World War II, Shostakovich emerged from the experience politically ambivalent and deeply suspicious of collective life—as did Kerouac, despite his inclination to engage the social and political debates of his times in early works such as *The Haunted Life*. In compositions such as the Eleventh Symphony, Shostakovich gave musical expression to this ambivalence—heightened as it was by the composer's need to survive as an artist amidst the censorious and stifling atmosphere of postwar Soviet society (which exposed his work to tremendous pressures and contributed to a long history of critical misunderstandings). Although the Eleventh Symphony commemorates the Soviet Revolution of 1905 with much bombast, it also expresses (in subtle fashion) its composer's doubts about the eventual direction of the Communist movement; indeed, later musicologists have connected its pessimistic passages to Shostakovich's misgivings regarding the Soviet Union's military response to the Hungarian uprising of 1956. Despite the well-documented demands of the Soviet authorities, Shostakovich made every attempt to resist clear-cut ideologies and party platforms in his music, as he hoped instead to memorialize all those whose lives and freedom had fallen victim to modern warfare and bureaucracy—something he did quite stirringly in his Seventh and Eighth Symphonies. For much of the Cold War era, Kerouac also refused to endorse cut-and-dry political ideologies, often to the consternation of cultural commentators and his literary colleagues. He tended to view such ideologies as forms of deferential obedience, capable of giving rise to fanaticism and mass destruction. As a result, Kerouac never once voted in an American election, nor did he ever claim a political affiliation or embrace any sort of conventionally identifiable politics. The roots of this ambivalence are perhaps to be found in his long-held attitudes toward war and death, as captured in the pages that follow.

Todd F. Tietchen
University of Massachusetts–Lowell

Suggestions for Further Reading

Brinkley, Alan. *Voices of Protest: Huey Long, Father Coughlin, and the Great Depression*. New York: Vintage, 1983.

Denning, Michael. *The Cultural Front: The Laboring of American Culture in the Twentieth Century*. London: Verso, 2011.

Dickstein, Morris. *Leopards in the Temple: The Transformation of American Fiction, 1945–1970*. Cambridge: Harvard University Press, 2002.

Johnson, Joyce. *The Voice Is All: The Lonely Victory of Jack Kerouac*. New York: Viking, 2012.

Kerouac, Jack. *On the Road: The Original Scroll*. New York: Penguin, 2008.

———. *Selected Letters, Volume 1: 1940–1956*. Edited by Ann Charters. New York: Penguin, 1996.

———. *The Sea Is My Brother*. Edited by Dawn Ward. Cambridge: Da Capo, 2012.

———. *The Town and the City*. New York: Harcourt Brace, 1950.

———. *Vanity of Duluoz*. New York: Coward-McCann, 1968.

McNally, Dennis. *Desolate Angel: Jack Kerouac, the Beat Generation, and America*. Cambridge: Da Capo, 2003.

Shostakovich, Dmitri. *Testimony: The Memoirs of Dmitri Shostakovich*. As related to and edited by Solomon Volkov. New York: Limelight Editions, 2006.

Notes on the Text

The following selections represent a significant addition to the public corpus of Kerouac's work. As Kerouac remains widely known for his playfulness with language—as well as his fondness for neologisms—I have made every attempt to transcribe the texts as they were originally written. I did make some minor grammatical adjustments, mostly for consistency of spelling and tense. Additionally, I removed a number of semicolons from the dialogue in *The Haunted Life* and replaced them with commas and periods as I saw fit. I viewed those semicolons as an early stylistic quirk that, given his own ear for spoken English, Kerouac would have later removed.

At times, portions of the material were not completely legible. When I felt confident enough in my guesswork, I placed the text in brackets [as such]. Those portions of text that I simply could not decipher have been indicated as such: [?]. Seeing as this is not a critical edition, I have resisted footnoting except in a few instances within Leo Kerouac's letters where it seemed unavoidable.

T. F. T.

Part I

The Haunted Life

"But, O the heavy change, now thou art gone,
Now thou art gone, and never must return!"
   —**Milton, "Lycidas"**

"And in myself too many things have perished which, I imagined, would last forever, and new structures have arisen, given birth to new sorrows and new joys which in those days I could not have foreseen, just as now the old are difficult of comprehension."
   —**Proust, *À la recherche du temps perdu***

"N'ous-je pas une fois une jeunesse
amiable, héroïque, fabuleuse, à écrire
sur des feuilles d'or, trop de chance!
par quel crime, par quelle erreur, aije
mérité ma faiblesse actuelle?"
   —**Rimbaud, *Une saison en enfer***

Part One

Home

I

"America isn't the same country anymore; it isn't even America anymore." Mr. Martin drew on his cigar with nodding and angry finality. "It's become a goddamn pesthole for every crummy race from the other side. America isn't America anymore. A white man can't walk down the street, or go in a restaurant, or do business, or do anything for that matter without having to mix up with these goddamn greasers from the other side."

On the couch across the unlit room, Peter Martin grinned over his cigarette.

"Crapule!" cried Mr. Martin, coughing smoke.

The light from the kitchen, where Aunt Marie was washing the dishes, fell into the dim front room where Mr. Martin was still coughing when his sister called from her dishpan, "Are you starting again?"

"You goddamn right I am!" he choked.

Peter reached for the radio dial to turn up the volume of a Benny Goodman record which had just begun. He repressed the impulse to announce the title of the number to the room in general; in a juke joint he would have cried it out triumphantly, announcing his knowledge of jazz.

"Wops!" resumed Mr. Martin, his voice thick. "Jews! Greeks! Niggers! Armenians, Syrians, every scummy race in the world. They've all come here, and they're still coming, and they'll keep on coming by the boatloads. Mark my word, you'll see the day when a real American won't have a chance to work and live decently in his own country, a day when ruin and bankruptcy will fall on this nation because all these damned foreigners will have taken everything over and made a holy mess of it."

Mr. Martin paused to puff quickly on his cigar. Peter was half listening. Aunt Marie was singing an aria from *Carmen* over her dishes in a small sweet voice.

"By God, that trip to New York opened my eyes plenty. I'd never dreamed things had reached this point . . . never! That city is crawling with dirty foreigners, and niggers! I've never seen so many niggers in all my life. A couple of days was all I needed to get the lay of the land. Black faces, greasy faces, all kinds of faces. I ask myself how can a white man live in that stinking town? What's happened to this country? Who is the cause of all this?"

"Roosevelt?" supplied Peter slyly.

"You don't need to mention it. You ought to know it as well as I do."

Peter leaned forward. "Oh I don't know, Pop . . . "

"Of course you don't know. You're only a kid. You haven't lived sixty years in this country. You didn't see America and work in America when it was really America . . . "

Peter blanked his cigarette.

"Now you take around here," went on the father from the dark corner, the cigar glowing an orange arc, "as it was fifty years ago, right in little Galloway, Massachusetts. We were all white people, working together. Your grandfather was only a carpenter, but he was an honest man, a hardworking man. None of this grasping and foreign conning for him. He got up in the morning, went to work for eleven hours a day, came home, ate supper, sat in the kitchen for a few hours thinking, and then went to bed. Like that! No shrewdness to him, just a straightforward, honest old boy. Ah God, he was . . . "

"What was Galloway like in those days?" prompted Peter.

"Well, like I was saying, we were all white people . . . a sprinkling of Irishmen, French-Canadians like ourselves, old English families, and a few Germans. You would have to see it to understand what I'm trying to tell you. We were . . . well, we were *honest*, the community was honest. Of course, there were a few thieves and cardsharps and peanut politicians, like you'll find anywhere in the world. But what I mean is, the general run of these people were on the up and up. Why, boy, it was a remarkable thing, now that I really look back on it. Life was a simple and quiet affair in those days; people were real and sincere and . . . friendly. They weren't ready to trim you the moment you turned your back, like these New York Jews; in those days it wasn't a matter of selling the cheapest goods for the highest price. It was, by God, a matter of selling the best possible. Look, you like those long-winded economic words, those they throw around at Boston College, well now, listen . . . competition in those days was based on who could put up the best goods for sale . . . the baker who made the best chocolate pie . . . and *not* on who could afford to undersell the others without regard to quality . . . "

"Why blame New York Jews for this change?" frowned Peter, intent on creating logic.

"You're right, I guess. It's not only the New York Jew. It's Jews all over the country, the Wop and all the others who bring with them from the other side ideas which are not American, and with it all their filthy ways . . . "

Aunt Marie had finished the dishes. She entered the front room, a statuesque lady with white hair braided close to her head, wearing a blue and white cotton housedress and a pair of worn house slippers. She sat in the chair by the window, where the last pink glow of dusk hovered behind the screen. June crickets were beginning their numberless chorale.

"These foreigners don't understand the real America . . . that's why they're so dangerous. They bring with them the old ways of Europe, the haggling cheesy manners, the crooked dealings, the damned smoke-screening . . . "

"What do you mean by smoke-screening?" interposed Peter.

"I mean just that! They say one thing, and they mean something else. They lie in your face. A man comes to a point where he can't figure out what they're after. If they want something, they don't come right out with it! They throw up a damned smoke-screen. They haven't got the guts, nor the honesty, to come out with it straight . . . "

Aunt Marie lit a Fatima and glazed placidly out the window. A commentator was speaking on the radio about the retreat of the Russians toward Moscow.

"These foreigners know which side their bread is buttered on. Roosevelt! The more foreigners, the more votes for him; he plays up to them, and they think it's wonderful. As for the rest of the American people, to hell with them! Roosevelt knows the real Americans won't be the fall guys to finance and support his dreams of dictatorship, so he turns to these foreigners, and they fall for it blissfully because that's all they knew back in the 'old country'—inflated balloons like Roosevelt! I tell you, the country is going to pot, and we're going to be dragged into the war by Roosevelt and the Jews and the British Empire! Mark my word! And someday, when people get a little more sense in their heads, they're going to catch on to Roosevelt's schemes." Mr. Martin rose to his feet, a tall spare man of sixty, white-haired and bespectacled, and moved across the dark room. "And he will go down in history as the greatest enemy to mankind America ever had!"

Mr. Martin was in the kitchen.

"Mark my word!" he shouted back, and slammed the bath-room door shut.

Aunt Marie sighed deeply. "He's getting worse year by year," she said, weighing her words with portent. "Worse and worse, year by year."

Peter got up and went over to the piano stool, grinning.

"Your poor mother was frightened to death of him, Petey. Even when he was a boy, he would rage around the house like a lion. Even father couldn't calm him down or tame him; he was always angry about something, always going around with a chip on his shoulder, always getting into trouble. I tell you, he's getting worse and worse, year by year . . ."

Peter struck a few keys on the old square back piano. He said, "Pop's always been a man with opinions, and he voices them good and loud, that's all."

"Well," said Aunt Marie, "you can say what you want, but I know Joe Martin, he's my brother, I've known him ever since he was so high, and I tell you he's never been all there, and he's getting worse year by year . . . "

Peter giggled and spun around in the piano stool to face the keyboard. He began to play chords, striking them at random, a discordant cat-on-the-keys performance. Aunt Marie turned on the chair lamp and peered at the pile of newspapers and magazines in a rack beneath an arm of Mr. Martin's easy chair. The announcer said it was eight-thirty.

Peter went to the radio and dialed for the baseball scores. Mr. Martin returned munching a last season's Mackintosh apple.

"I'm listening to *Fibber McGee and Molly* at nine o'clock," he told his son, grinning. "Until then, the radio is yours . . . "

"Wow! Teddy Williams got three more hits today," cried Peter.

Searching around for his reading glasses, Mr. Martin said: "He's a good one, that Williams."

Peter returned to the couch and lit another cigarette. Aunt Marie looked up from her *Saturday Evening Post*.

"Petey, don't smoke so much. You smoke almost as much as Wesley used to . . . "

"Did he smoke a lot?"

"My lord, yes. The doctor told him to stop smoking many times, but he never did. For all we know he may be consumptive by now . . . "

Mr. Martin looked up, frowning. His eyes were dark. "Smoke? That fool kid *drinks* like ten men."

"That's what they teach them at sea. There's no harder life than the sailor's . . . "

Martin went on, ignoring his sister: "He was a high school punk when he started drinking. I remember one afternoon I stopped in at McTigue's bar on Woolcott Street, and there was my own sixteen-year-old son sitting drunk at the bar, with a dozen empty shot glasses around him . . . smoking a cigarette. It didn't faze him that I happened to catch him . . . " Mr. Martin's voice was softened in recollection. "By God, Marie, he was a strange little tyke . . . a strange lad . . . "

Peter listened with soft wonder. Whenever they spoke about Wesley he felt that way, sad and filled with mystery. He had a brother, surely, Wesley Martin; but Wesley Martin was a dark and haunting legend. Wesley had not been home for nine or ten years. He was a seaman. Occasionally, a letter would find its way to Galloway, always written in a strange yet simple script; always worded simply, yet strangely. Peter shook his head slowly, puzzled.

"How old is he by now?" asked Mr. Martin, turning a suddenly drawn and helpless face on Aunt Marie.

She knew it instantly, but performed a little ritual of recollection, counting on her fingers and mumbling. "He'll be twenty-seven in December. He left home in the Spring of 1932, that will be ten years come next Spring . . . "

"And you were just a little lad, Petey," said Mr. Martin, gazing on his son blankly.

"I was ten years old. Tell me, Pop, why did Wesley leave home? I mean, was there any particular reason, or was it just . . . that business about Helen Copley . . . "

"That was reason enough for Wesley." Mr. Martin relit his cigar slowly. "He was driving, so he felt responsible for everything that happened. The Copley girl's face was smashed up. Young Wilson lost a couple of fingers. Wesley himself wasn't hurt much, which made it worse for his conscience. He was a sensitive lad . . . "

Aunt Marie leaned forward in her chair. "Why, Helen Copley

looks just as good as ever today. Her scars healed up in a year's time."

"Yep, I guess . . . " Mr. Martin sighed heavily. "I guess Wesley's leaving home was just a matter of time anyway. The accident, and the remorse that followed it, only saw to it that he went off a few years ahead of schedule. Restless boy, he was, like all the Martins. Why, my brother Frank . . . "

"Helen Copley's married today and has children. She has a lovely husband. I wrote and told Wesley a dozen times, but he doesn't seem to listen."

Aunt Marie bit her lip and went on. "He had no true reason for leaving a good home and going off as he did—at seventeen, for the love of God—a child . . . "

"It was in the cards," said Mr. Martin. "He was restless, like all the Martins. And I guess he's done alright for himself . . . those seaman make good money and live in the open. By God," Mr. Martin grinned slyly, "by God, I've always wanted to travel around the world in a freighter myself."

"But it's so dangerous now," objected Aunt Marie. "Don't you read the papers? The Germans are sinking all the ships, American or otherwise. Soon there may be war and . . . "

"Wesley'll get more pay," piped in Peter, almost enthusiastically. "They pay them big bonuses for taking the submarine risk."

"I don't care how much they pay them," insisted Aunt Marie in the face of the grinning males, both of whom were now launched on thoughts of the sea. "Human life is more important than money. I expect Wesley to come home someday, the poor child, when he gets a chance; and I want him to come home all in one piece. I'm only saying what his poor mother would have said."

In the silence that followed, in the middle of a pause on the radio, a large June moth smashed headlong into the screen and dropped in a dizzy flutter on the windowpane. The McCarthy dog barked from down the street. The Western sky was a cool pale blue, made alive by one dazzling silver star.

"He's seeing the world," went on Mr. Martin, extending a monologue he'd been having with himself. "That's more than I can say for myself. Selling insurance in this town wasn't so bad in the old days. I liked it. But now," he smashed the arm of the chair with a big fist, "now Galloway's getting to be a crumbhole! Every store downtown that was ever worth a cent or two is now being run by Jews! And if not Jews, Greeks and Armenians! The Wops are pouring in from Lawrence and Haverhill! I tell you, I'm glad Wesley cleared out of this town; sometimes I wonder if he wasn't the smartest of the bunch."

"Don't start that again," cried Aunt Marie almost savagely.

Martin stared at her as though she were some indescribable creature from Mars.

"Women," he yelled, "never knew and never will know a damned thing! Right under your big nose this country is going to the dogs, and you want me to shut up! Good God Almighty, your brains don't add up, I think, to more than a teaspoonful of sawdust!"

"You don't have to yell!"

"Why not? This is my house, isn't it? If the neighbors don't like it, they can all go to hell!"

Peter walked to the kitchen for a glass of water and snickered gleefully.

"You can't sell these foreigners a policy," his father was shouting, "without having to sign your life's blood away. They don't know what a man's word means—where they come from everybody is so damn dishonest and downright crooked they all have to sleep with one eye open. They don't know a thing about America and the way people live here, and yet here they come! Here they come by the boatloads! Why the hell didn't they stay in their cheesy European towns? Why the hell don't they go back? When will they learn that the American people don't want them here? Will we have to ship them back, ass baggage and all, before they find out we don't want them here?"

Chuckling mildly at the outburst, Aunt Marie now lit another Fatima and settled back with her reading. Peter was standing in the doorway.

Martin suddenly remembered. "What time is it?"

"Three minutes past nine."

"Fibber McGee!" cried Mr. Martin, jumping out of the chair. "Missed part of it!"

Peter's kid sister Diane came in from the front porch carrying her high school books. She dashed across the room toward the living room, calling: "Aunt Marie, did you make some lemonade tonight?"

"It's on the icebox."

Diane, in a neat blouse and skirt, her brown hair falling straight down to the shoulders, rummaged furiously through the living room buffet drawer. Peter watched her from the doorway, toothpick in mouth.

"What you looking for?"

"None of your business."

Annoyed, Peter said: "Huh! Big stuff now that you're finished with Junior year." Diane did not reply.

Aunt Marie called: "Diane, I thought you said rehearsals would end in time for supper?"

"Didn't! Miss Merriom wanted us to make up for lost time. I ate at Jacqueline's house."

"Quiet!" yelled Mr. Martin. "I want to hear this program."

Diane emerged from the living room with a dangle of blue ribbon. She said, "Rose said she was coming with Billie tonight."

"I know," mumbled Aunt Marie. "She should be here any minute."

"Rose!" exploded Mr. Martin.

"Yes, Rose, my daughter Rose. Did you ever hear of her?" taunted Aunt Marie.

"She'll bring the kid! I'll never hear the program! Goddamnit! He cries like a baby!"

"He is a baby."

Peter, grinning, went out to the screened porch and sat in the creaking hammock. It was a chilly night, thick with odorous dew, swarming with stars and cricket sounds. The radio blared behind; across the street, in the cluster of trees where he had played as a boy, fireflies blinked erratically. Over the cooling fields toward the Merrimac River a train whistle howled.

ROSE LARGAY, Aunt Marie's only daughter, came at quarter past nine with her four-year-old son, Billie, and her neighbor, Maggie Sidelinker, a newlywed bride. Mr. Martin took refuge on the screened porch with Diane's portable radio; and Peter escaped up to his room, turned on the reading lamp and slumped in a sagging leather easy chair with *Patterns for Living*. It was hot in the room from the latent heat of a sunblazing June afternoon. A

June bug raged at the bay window screen. Peter could hear the portable from the porch where his father sat, an exile from the front room with its flurry of gossip and smells of sticky lollipops and women.

"Young Writer Remembering Chicago." Peter read slowly, admiring the young Halper's tragic sense of youth and lonesomeness. "My arms are heavy, I've got the blues; there's a locomotive in my chest and that's a fact."

Peter leaned back in his chair, closed his eyes, and tried to visualize the young Albert Halper in a cheap rooming house in Manhattan, his arms heavy, his spirit driven and wearied by a heavy, vital drive. Someday, he, Peter, would rent a cheap room in Manhattan, and sit in a chair to stare at the flecked plaster wall. There would be the fundamental challenges of reality! There he would be pitted against the problems of the spirit (and of the stomach), a lonely youth, friendless in the great city, whose chief occupation would be that of ferreting out whatever beauty was left to be seen and smelled and touched and felt. A mission of that sort, appealing to the romantic instincts he knew he had inherited from something essentially American in his boyhood, held a billion fertile possibilities. He must try that sometime! There were many jobs to be had in New York . . . all the way down to dishwashing. Suppose he were to go to New York someday, get a job washing dishes in a big hotel, and it turned out that his fellow dishwashers were (1) a discontented Communist, (2) a careless vagabond from New Orleans, and (3) a young artist seeking to sell his watercolors. What a world of promise New York must hold!

Here in Galloway—

Peter kneeled at the bay window and looked out at the summer night. Down by the corner the streetlight shone, illuminating the front porch of Dick Sheffield's house. Beyond, over a cluster of homes partly buried in heavy oak and maple foliage—with soft squares of gold light falling from parlor windows onto green lawns—in the hazy summer night distance, the lights of downtown Galloway glowed, topped by the gangling red-lighted frame of the WGLH radio station antenna.

Straight across the street, a cluster of trees, and beyond, the field where the boys played ball, rolling toward the railroad tracks and the river. Silent night fields, with perhaps a couple or two strolling in search of thick bramble.

Down toward the other corner, where the streetlamp illumined a heavy, rustling mass of foliage and threw a faint glow across the street to the rambling McCarthy house. Light from the McCarthy porch.

Such was Galloway. What could a man do in a burg like this? What cultural opportunities flowered, what learning and art flourished here?

The smell?

Field smell, flower smell, and the smell of cooling black tar in the night. The air misty and drooping with its weight of odors, the river's moist gust of breeze, the rotting cherry blossoms in the backyard, and the strong green smell of tree leaves trembling against the bay window screen.

The sounds?

Peter held his breath to listen . . . the voices of the McCarthys drinking lemonade on their porch. The radio next door, Mary Quigley and her girlfriend from Riverside St., dancing to a soothing Bob Eberly ballad in the living room littered with new and old recordings. The McCarthy dog barking at the kids who slink by in the dark playing gangsters or cowboys or maybe war.

Again the train . . . moving north to Montreal . . . howling long and hoarse, a mournful night sound . . .

Silence now for a moment . . . and the river hush, and the trembling of tree leaves. Far across the field, over the tracks and over to the boulevard across the river, where the cars move endlessly back and forth from the city to the ice cream road stands, the fried clam restaurants, the pink-lit roadhouses all crowded with shuffling dancers, the faint beep of klaxons returns.

Now the sound of crickets, and that old bullfrog from the reeds in Haley's Creek. And Pop's Fibber McGee program from below on the porch, the audience crashing with sudden laughter. And Aunt Marie, Cousin Rose, her little brat, her friend, and Diane bubbling about trifles in the parlor; high laughter . . .

As such, Galloway—

PETER GOT UP off his knees and stood surveying his room, idly lighting a fresh cigarette. It was a small but useful room, useful in the sense that it fitted his personality. Peter was the "den-type." He wanted a place to retreat to, a place—a room—containing certain necessities which he felt, as perhaps an Alaskan trapper might feel, would be near at hand in an emergency unpredictable in length. Here were stored his rations of the spirit . . . books, a typewriter, paper, pencils and pens, envelopes, old letters, recent letters, mementos of childhood and boyhood, scrapbooks containing pertinent clippings and notebooks containing impertinent remarks, clusters of junk bearing no relation to one another and long out of purpose—pieces of colored crayon and chalk, marbles and migs, buttons, Yale locks, rolls of tape and string, seashore rocks and shells, matchbooks filled with assortments of tacks and small magnets and bottle caps, pieces of elastic and bunting, empty inkbottles, old keys: all the minutiae a lad collects and, when he is fortunate enough, keeps, as a trinket-link with the always golden past.

Of a more singular nature, Peter here also hoarded the cunning achievements of his boyhood—a large slat-ribbed box overflowing with notebooks and stacks of paper now yellowed and crinkling. These notebooks contained systematic records of his imaginary "events" . . . a complicated system of nations, and their wars and sports, with appropriate native historian's bombast, mellow sentimentality, elaborate detail, and proud, neat script. Thousands of names were buried in this slat-ribbed box, names culled from phonebooks for personalities of high or low estate conjured from the mind of boyhood . . . kings of nations, the official maps of which were preserved in great cracking scrolls; giants of the battlefield whose achievements dwarfed, as can be expected, the Napoleons; athletes of mellow renown, whose exploits were eked out in a hundred thousand hours bent over an arrangement of marbles and sticks and stacks of paraphernalia incomprehensible, of course, to anyone but Peter Martin forever. Here were files upon files, painstakingly accurate, recording forever in the boy's mind the fruits of a weird but original imagination.

And then there were the first watercolors, stiff landscapes, the inevitable island with palm leaning over the surf at sunset, the riotously green trees and mad blues and purples of sky and water. And the first novel . . . printed by hand in a notebook, a hundred pages on the adventures of "Jack" with illustrations. And the countless strips of cartoon drawings, extending adventure upon adventure to the square-jawed, pipe-smoking, angularly built hero, "Bart Lawson" or "Secret Operative K-11."

Too, the attempts at humor . . . the morbidly ridiculous little cartoon character who forever gets in trouble and is not funny at all, but somehow vaguely insane. All of this, and more . . . piles of handwritten "daily newspapers," telling of the news in a loud and insolent voice; containing editorials which somehow resemble real grown-up editorials, strangely enough, in that they strain to fill up the allotted space and say nothing worth one line of the news itself. And, of course, diaries abounding with temperament, stoic admissions of ennui, and gleefully excited eyewitness reports of flood, fire, and hurricane.

Along with this—and everything else—Peter had stored in his den all the old toys, bats-balls-and-gloves, puppy love presents and rings, and photographs necessary to round out the wholeness of his past.

Now, on top of this stratum with its deep undercurrents—fecund and psychological—of boyhood, Peter had and was amassing a new private civilization. He had a radio-phonograph, complete with a growing collection of classical, swing, and jazz records. The music covered a wide field, from Gershwin with his romantic hint of far Manhattan, or back to Benny Goodman and Artie Shaw—whose rhythms excited the present younger generation and prepared them, or at least Peter and a few scattered others, for the serious side of the new music, call it jazz or swing, which culminated in the highly complicated and quite profound melodic improvisations of soloists Coleman Hawkins, Roy Eldridge, and Lester Young to mention a few, Negroes all, to whom the music actually belonged—and over to Delius, whose haunting lyrics struck Peter at first hearing (something compatibly mystic in his nature) and paved the way for an appreciation of like moderns, Debussy, Tchaikovsky, Rachmaninoff, Shostakovich; which in turn developed the senses, groomed and prepared them, for the masters themselves—Beethoven, Mozart, Schubert, Brahms.

Foremost on Peter's bookshelf, that is standing on the top in an elite group, were Thoreau, Homer, the Bible, Melville's *Moby Dick*, *Ulysses*, Thomas Wolfe, Shakespeare, Whitman, *Faust*, Dostoevsky, and Tolstoy. On the next shelf, Peter had relegated several authors of more than passing interest to him, but of less than passing interest, he feared, to Homer-Bible-Shakespeare and company. These flickering lights included William Saroyan, Sherwood Anderson, Albert Halper, and a few other whimsical favorites such as Rupert Brooke, Carl Sandburg, and Edna St. Vincent Millay—and the Hemingway–Fitzgerald–Dos Passos group.

In a pile on the desk lay Peter's periodical reading, a smattering of liberal publications running from *The Nation* on—or back, or up or down—to New York's daily *PM* and over the side to the *New Masses* and whatever few copies of the *Daily Worker* he was able to pick up. These he read a great deal puzzled—but he read with intent to learn. He mistrusted political texts, preferred glancing simultaneously at two divergently opinionated organs to get each side's opinion of the other, and thus achieve a glimpse of motives, split propaganda from fact, and try to understand the issue as it was. In this vein, he often sought opinions on the same subject in the two papers *PM* and Hearst's *Boston Daily Record*. Here he found people at each other's throats and wondered mildly—with his eye searching for motives, even for the vital motive behind the motives—what warranted such agitation.

Above the old working desk were emblems also representative of Peter's present life—a Boston College banner and a brilliant constellation of track medals of honor. This display, sophomoric though it was, served mainly to identify—in this strange bedlam of a room—a phase of Peter's life. The room's purpose justified the conceit. It told the legend of his scholarship at Boston College, partly athletic and partly scholastic, while the large "44" indicated he had completed his freshman year.

These, in part, were the objects which lived in Peter's room, and which more or less manifested his life up to the summer of 1941. On to Africa as an explorer, and return with a Kenyan's spear, and he would lean it in a corner to show for that. With satisfaction and a pride touched with humor, Peter thus surveyed his room.

It was furnished not the way he would have desired, however; it bore Aunt Marie's daily touch. The wallpaper suggested a nursery or a playroom, it was that bright and flowery. The new bookcase she had replaced the old brown one with had that new varnished maple look that seemed somehow unintellectual—more, unscholarly. The curtains sang with sunshine and joy, the quilted rug before the dresser needed only an angora kitten playing with a ball of darning.

But the old brown leather easy chair was still there, and the littered desk with the stuffed pigeonholes, the dusty big typewriter, the spare simple floor lamp, the old-fashioned living room chair with wooden back and leather seat, and the old iron bedstead with its brown paint chipping off to show an older integument of scholar's brown—these remained; and somehow, Aunt Marie's light and cheerful touch did not do *too* much harm. Her bright, neat spirit hovered over the stuffy brownness, vowing dust and disrepair could never turn this room, in spite of its stiff bookshelvean resistance, into a Faustian dungeon. This was a secure thought for one who lived in, but was not responsible entirely for, a room.

2

"Petey!"

Peter was lying on his back on the bed, staring at the dark slanting ceiling, almost dozing.

"Petey!"

It was Garabed calling from the side yard, nineteen-year-old Garabed Tourian who still called for Peter from the side yard with hands cupped to mouth as he had been doing for ten years.

Peter ran to the small window facing the Quigley house next door and pressed his nose against the screen. Garabed was standing in the moonlight below, slender and casual in white shirt-sleeves, smoking a cigarette.

"Hey Garabed!" greeted Peter. "What time is it?"

"About ten-thirty I guess."

Peter yawned: "What are you doing?"

"Nothing. Come on out . . ."

Peter stretched his arms: "Where shall we go?"

"Anywhere," said Garabed. "Come on."

Peter turned on the floor lamp and found his cigarettes. He picked up a worn copy of the *Pocket Book of Verse*, turned out the light, and went downstairs. His father was back in the front room listening to a mystery thriller over the big Philco radio. Rose and the others had gone home.

"Your Armenian is outside," said Mr. Martin.

Peter went into the kitchen. Aunt Marie sat at the table sipping a coke over the *Boston Daily Record*, intent on Walter Winchell.

"Don't come home at six o'clock tomorrow morning," she said.

Peter mumbled, "I won't," and opened the refrigerator door. He picked up two bottles of Coca-Cola and went out the back way. Diane was in the entry replacing a mop in a pail.

"Kewpie was sick again. You better take that damned old cat down to the Humane Society."

"Don't be stupid," cried Peter with annoyance. "He's sick from something he ate. That's cat's healthier and younger than you are." Diane was standing peeved, with arms akimbo, when Peter gently closed the door in her face.

He could hear her yelling: "It's *your* old cat. Clean up after him yourself!"

Garabed had plucked a rose from the Quigley bush and twined the stem in his black hair. He leaned loosely against a dark tree trunk.

"Here," said Peter, handing over a coke. "Hell, I guess I've been sleeping. I was reading Halper at nine o'clock or so . . . "

They sat on the front porch steps. The moon had risen over the trees down the street, shrinking and whitening as it rose.

"Oh moon, thy sideways sadness," quoted Garabed with a dour smile. "O compassionate moon!"

Peter grinned: "Don't make fun of my great poem."

Garabed turned an olive-skinned, dark-eyed face on the other. "I'm not making fun of it. I think it's good. I'm quoting it. You know I have the only existing copy in my possession." He smiled, lifting the bottle to drink. "'Supreme Reality' . . . a poem in four parts, by Peter Martin. It's good, Pierre. An ardent lyrical outburst. I cherish it."

Peter finished his coke and set it on the steps. "It's not good poetry, certainly. It's a riot of free verse. Too much Whitman in it."

"That's alright—you're a prose writer. I'm the verse writer on this street."

"Dubious distinctions for North Street."

"I spent the whole afternoon," said Garabed, "in the library reading the *Encyclopedia Americana*. God, what a job it would be to read the whole thing! I spent two hours reading about Birmingham, Alabama, alone. Steel manufacturing. Cotton . . . "

"What's the idea?"

"I don't know. I had nothing to do. I went to a show at five o'clock, one of those God-awful Republic Pictures. I don't know why I did that either. Coming out, I met George Breton. He says not to forget Saturday afternoon . . . baseball or something. I don't know, I'm in a strange listless mood today. What did you do?"

"I had to write those letters I told you about, to the people at Boston College."

Garabed took the rose out of his hair and stood up, smiling deeply.

"Let's go for a walk," he said.

Peter threw the empty bottles on the hammock and they started down the street.

"How's your father?" grinned Garabed.

"Same as ever, Bed. A Coughlinite at heart. Part of his thinking is logical, I suppose . . . "

"For instance?"

"That part a sixty-year-old New England insurance salesman of commodious means should have . . . in contrast with that part two fresh kids like you and I should not have."

"What's wrong with our thinking?" laughed Garabed defensively, flourishing the rose.

"On the whole, it's good. But we haven't *lived*. We have only thought . . . "

"Pete, for God's sake, where did you pick *that* up? You sound like my own father!"

"I don't know—I've been thinking. I hate to be a fresh intellectual who scorns his elders. There's something . . . oddly inorganic about it, or something."

"Inorganic?" screamed Garabed.

"Well, anyway, what should we do tonight?"

"I'm disillusioned tonight," said Garabed. "I don't care what I do . . . "

"What disillusioned you: Birmingham, Alabama?"

Garabed screamed again: "No! Claire's letter caused my disillusionment. Birmingham, Alabama was a reaction."

"What's Claire got to say?"

"In my last letter I told her she resembled a lovely brown swallow. She replied I had stolen the phrase from Swinburne's 'Itylus' . . . "

"Come to the point. What hurt you?"

Garabed raised his chin and looked down: "I am not hurt."

"You are too. Is she sore about anything? That night in Boston, for instance, when I got you drunk?"

"God, no, she's forgotten all about that—anyway, she never did mind. No, she's peeved because I didn't go to see her last week. To tell you the truth, I don't care. This summer all I want to do is loll in the sun and read and swim and be silent. These amours of mine wear me out emotionally. God! I feel like a Dostoevsky character every time I mingle with the Boston crowd. I'm vowing a summer of silence. I must be silent even now . . . "

Peter laughed and pushed Garabed away: "You crazy Armenian. How you've changed. I can remember when you were drooling and your main concern was how to outwit George away from his marbles."

They walked toward the railroad tracks, slashing through the tall grass. Peter chuckled: "Remember when you were my Hollywood reporter? You'd come to the yard and yell out my name and I'd come to the window and there you stood with your deadline."

Garabed smiled sadly: "I remember, I remember . . . "

"Our one subscriber was poor Paul Dubois. We didn't even know he was dying of cancer . . . "

"I remember Paul Dubois. I'll never forget the night he was sitting in the hammock in his backyard telling me about his trip to Cleveland or someplace. Poor dying youth. He used to buy your paper . . . "

"Five cents a copy," recollected Peter.

" . . . *and* read it, just to please us, two snot-nosed kids. I'll bet he'd have made a great man. He had the power of compassion."

Peter placed a hand on Garabed's thin shoulder. "Power of compassion . . . the essence of Tourianism."

"Certainly," smiled Garabed. Then, gravely: "The greatest men were those who had that power, sympathetic and understanding men . . . Christ, St. Francis, Dostoevsky, Lenin."

"I remember, I remember," mocked Peter mildly.

They crossed the shining, still warm railroad tracks and descended through a tangle of bushes toward a clearing by the water's edge where sand had been spread to make a swimming beach.

"You know that as well as I do," remonstrated Garabed. "These were the men who suffered, the compassionate heroes of mankind, the lovers of humanity . . . "

Garabed's rose burned an otherworldly red in the moonlight.

"It's a beautiful thought, Bed, but it won't withstand . . . "

"Won't withstand . . . what?"

"I don't know." Peter sat in the sand and flicked his cigarette over the beach into the water. "Your creed is like some lovely fragile thing that can be swept away like a fume with the first breeze . . . compassion is not really a power, it's more a weakness."

"Lovely and fragile," echoed Garabed. "Pete, for God's sake, life is lovely and fragile; look at this rose . . . "

"I know," Peter grinned. "Your compassion is no stronger. It will die . . . soon. There are forces so much stronger. I'm not commending them, but they will win out, these stronger forces."

"Christ's compassion," hissed Garabed, "has had more effect on the Western world than any other man's force . . . be it Napoleon's shrewdness or Bismarck's whatever-he-had! Besides, the same applies to the East, where Buddha's teachings live on."

"Poor Garabed. I don't mean that. I'm talking about you yourself. You're defenseless. You don't dare to read Freud for fear of upsetting your emotional habits. Dostoevsky terrifies you with his Slavic portraits that remind you too much of yourself. You fear ugliness, you chase beauty and embrace it."

"So?"

"So someday, something ugly and real will happen. Compassion will not help. Strength you will need, but you won't have it. You'll crack."

"Pierre," purred Garabed, exhibiting the rose, "I'll still have my sapphire."

Peter piled some sand to make a pillow and lay back. "Your sapphire. That's just a symbol of beauty. Ugliness, when it storms you, will destroy your sapphire and leave you a hollow shell. Boo!"

Across the river, the headlights of cars felt their way along the boulevard. The air smelled of river mud.

"You're wrong, Peter, completely wrong. Don't start getting 'prim glacial on definitions' with me. You must have been reading the *Partisan Review* anyway."

Peter laughed.

"Don't laugh. Don't you realize the Great Liberal Movement is founded on compassion? . . ."

"Oh God you make it all so beautifully simple, Garabed, I only hope you're right . . ."

"Don't you realize that progress, from Prometheus, down the ages to . . . to Lenin, has been the work of great and good men, men of faith? These men were not cynics, they believed in the soul of mankind, in the brotherhood of man. Look at Billie Saroyan!"

"He's your Armenian conspirator . . ."

"Billie is a great and good writer, I don't care what some people say. He's compassionate, he feels for people and for the principles of the brotherhood of man; and besides," grinned Garabed, "he writes such beautiful and sad stuff. Remember? That story called 'The Warm, Quiet Valley of Home'? Saroyan and his cousin go out hunting and don't kill anything. Let us salute the absent inhabitants of the world, his cousin said. That's a noble thought, Saroyan said. They lifted their guns to their shoulders and pointed at nothing in the sky. To the dead, his cousin said. They fired the guns . . . the sound was half-crazy and half-tragic. To Kerop, Saroyan said. They fired again. To Harlan, his cousin said, and again they fired. To everyone who once lived on this earth and died, his cousin said. They fired the guns . . . ”

“That was wonderful,” Peter nodded.

“Oh, and remember . . . ‘it’s the poor breaking heart.’ He means life’s sadness. Saroyan has heart, Pete, that’s why I love him . . . ”

Peter, lying on his back, was staring up at a skyful of rich, nodding stars. The river rustled behind Garabed’s words.

“‘There’s a barrel-organ caroling across a golden street in the city where the sun sinks low . . . ’ By God, Saroyan could have written that. He has that eye that picks out the tragi-comic everywhere, the beautiful and the sad. Pete, honestly, it will be one of the great moments of my life when I meet him.”

“It would be for me too.”

“We’ve *got* to meet him, honestly. Someday, we’ll sit right down in some old jalopy and drive right out to Fresno, California.” Garabed chuckled enthusiastically. “What a mad time we’d have! We’d introduce ourselves simply and classily as Garabed Tourian and Peter Martin from Galloway, Massachusetts, a couple of young writers. Saroyan would be delighted to see us . . . ”

“Poor, poor, poor,” grinned Peter. “Garabed, your ambition is so pricelessly uncomplicated.”

Garabed lighted a cigarette. He said, “I just happened to think about Russia. I am now unhappy. God!”

Peter sat up: “What a retreat . . . it’s awful.”

“I wrote a few lines about the Russian youth at the front, last night in my room . . . ”

“I’m afraid for Moscow,” began Peter.

“Remember our pact?” asked Garabed with a wan smile. “Moscow on a Sunday afternoon—”

"A gray Sunday afternoon—"

"Yes, a cloudy one; and vodka in a bare room, looking out over the rooftops of the city . . . Anyway, I wrote a few lines."

"What were they?"

"Poor Russian youth," mumbled Garabed, not listening. "Poor kids. Isn't it really awful? I mean, right at this very moment while we sit by the river, they are dying . . . they are dying . . . "

"For what?"

"They are dying in the night . . . they cry: 'Why must we die in the night encarmined in our own blood?'—those are the lines. Oh, hell, Pete I don't know for what . . . I think of the German youth . . . "

"The little brownshirters?"

"I'm trying to look at it sans politics."

"I don't know either, Bed. I'll wager it's more sensible to write poems about it than try to analyze it politically. Who knows? If we get into it, look out . . . I mean, goodbye Garabed, goodbye Peter."

Garabed leaned back and clasped his knees.

"Maybe," grinned Peter, "if we listen and be quiet, we can hear the guns . . . "

They were silent. The train, miles away, wailed a long, dim cry.

"Same old sleepy America," went on Peter. "Look at that self-same old river. Do you remember when we first dared to swim all the way across? . . . Years ago . . . I think we were in grammar school. But I was always a better swimmer than you . . . "

Garabed was sifting sand through his fingers.

"A wind is rising," he said, "and the rivers flow. Remember? . . . From Wolfe."

"Yes. I'll remember. I'll remember . . . "

The train was only a mile away. They could hear the rails back of the bushes sing with the oncoming roar.

LATER—

At John O'Keefe's all-night lunch cart.

"Pete, does the family ever hear from your brother?" Garabed had just finished a fourth hamburger and was assiduously wiping his mouth with a paper napkin.

"Wesley?" Peter frowned. "He sent a Christmas card last year from Tampico. Doesn't say much . . ."

Garabed's eyes seemed to enlarge as they moistened. He didn't drop his head, but gazed into Peter's eyes. "It's a shame," he whispered, contorting his mouth.

Peter repressed a grin. "He's doing alright for himself."

"I remember Wesley," ignored Garabed. "I mean, I remember him vividly . . . One night, he was walking down North Street— when I was nine years old. He was sad, and I stood watching him. I remember because it was April and it was raining. The raindrops were falling by the streetlight, straight down. Wesley wore a raincoat, a black one, and no hat. His hair was wet and it hung over his eyes. I was coming home form the drugstore with some aspirins or something for my sister Esther. I said, 'Hiya Wes!'—and he looked at me sadly—Oh! I'll never forget it! He said, 'Hello'—just that, not ingratiating or anything like that, just a simple, sad, sincere hello—and he went on up the street . . ."

The jukebox began to play. Officer Haley came in, wiping his gaunt red face with a blue polka dot handkerchief; he sat at the counter and warded off a fly with his hand. The overhead fan blew down a gray forelock as he momentarily removed his hat to wipe the band.

"That was a few weeks before he left." Garabed dipped down for a slurp of coffee, rose: "Isn't it strange, Pierre, that I should remember like that? Of course, I can also remember all the obvious things: the time Wesley was in that crackup on the Boulevard, the time he pitched a no-hit no-run game in Twi League, the time he threw a stuffed chair out of the second story window of your house because it was burning and the whole neighborhood stood around watching him as he dumped pails of water from above . . . God! Those things are easy to remember . . . "

"I know," nodded Peter. "Like the time he bought that old '28 Chevy and fixed it up in our backyard. Damn it, Bed, he got up at six o'clock that morning—it was during Summer vacation—and began to work on it. I was his assistant. 'Give me that cotter pin, hand over that wrench' . . . all day long. At noon he had the whole motor disemboweled and lying all over the yard. At dusk, he had 'er together again—and the whole neighborhood nauseous from the exhaust . . . He was a natural. A wonderful mechanic."

"I remember he worked at that Socony station near the bridge." Garabed's voice softened again. "He used to come home in his mechanic's overalls, smoking a cigarette, a slim dark-eyed fellow."

"Yes," said Peter, "he had my father's eyes, and his build too. I take after my mother, they tell me: blue eyes, heavier physique. Still and all—" Peter sighed heavily—"Wesley's been everywhere. Singapore, Liverpool, New Orleans, Hawaii—all over to hell and gone. What a life, the sea. Dick Sheffield and I used to dream of running away from home and going to sea—once we got so far as Boston, mind you, and prowled around the waterfront all night . . . "

Garabed stabbed a crust of bread with a toothpick.

"I still think it's a shame, what I mean is, it *really* is a shame. Homeless, wandering . . . Don't you see what sort of life that is? Loneliness, loneliness . . . And poor Wesley never comes home."

Peter waved a hand. "What is there in Galloway for a guy like him? He's an anachronism—he should have gone West with the forty-niners, or sailed with Hanno or something. He has no roots, really, because he deliberately starved them. He's left nothing behind, no mark of his sixteen or seventeen years in Galloway, and no regrets either . . . " Peter puckered his brow. "The truth is, as you know, I haven't seen him since I was so high, and so I don't know what sort of a fellow he's grown into. I can't even clearly remember him as he was ten years ago, and certainly not at all from the mature point of view. So I don't know . . . But it is my idea that Wesley is doing what he wants to do—I mean, he is no exile, he's not forced into that kind of life, of loneliness as you say. He's just not the kind of guy who marries and settles down, so-called. He's not domesticated. I guess he's just a sailor, that's all. We can't understand it because we're just a couple of mama's boys . . . "

Garabed shook his head slowly.

"I still think it's terrible," he said. "Why—" Garabed fluttered his hand, a futile gesture to indicate all he believed in—"why, it's tragic . . . and beautiful, but beautiful in a frightful way. Horrible! It wouldn't be so bad for me, I would have my sapphire. But Wesley . . . he looked so sad and lost that night, long ago. Hello, he said. Somehow, I feel he is still the same, hasn't changed a bit. Hello. Sad hellos all around the world, lost in the rain . . . "

Peter laughed and pushed Garabed's shoulder back.

"Okay, Tourian. Save that for your collected works."

Garabed smiled sadly.

Peter mussed the black curly hair. "Come on, you crazy Armenian, let's go home."

UNDER A STREETLAMP at the corner of Wild and Henderson streets, Garabed Tourian—

"'So we'll go no more a-roving so late into the night, though the heart be still as loving, and the moon be still as bright . . .'"

Peter interrupting—

"'You to the left and I to the right, for the ways of men must sever; well may it be for a day or a night, well may it be forever—'"

"Oh Pete, where the hell's your taste?" Garabed raised his voice to its original pitch: "'Though the night was made for loving'—Platonic, of course—'and the day returns too soon, we'll go no more a-roving by the light of the moon . . .'"

"What time is it?"

"About four—listen to this: 'Forlorn! The very word is like a bell to toll me back from thee to my sole self! . . . Adieu! the fancy cannot cheat so well as she is famed to do, deceiving elf. Adieu! adieu! thy plaintive anthem fades past the near meadows, over the still stream, up the hill-side—'"

There was a burble of sound behind Garabed's cries, coming from an open window across the street. Someone was shouting in a rasping, sarcastic male voice.

" . . . and go to bed, or I'll call the police by Christ. Go back to where you belong!" There was stunned silence.

In answer, Garabed dropped on one knee and addressed the man in the window.

"I'll tell you where we belong . . . 'The Isles of Greece, the isles of Greece! Where burning Sappho loved and sung, where grew the arts of war and peace, where Delos rose and Phoebus sprung . . .'"

"I'm coming down, you wise bastards!" The voice came almost quietly, thick with angry humiliation, slow with threat.

"'Eternal summer gilds them yet,'" replied Garabed, as Peter began to snicker uncontrollably. "'But all, except their sun, is set . . .'" He knelt there, under the streetlamp, the far side of the street iron gray with the false dawn.

For a moment, the man was stunned. Then, with weary decision—as though he were being assigned, thanklessly, to a task that must be done—he said: "Alright . . . I'm coming down." The window was closed, slowly, a sound filling the silence that followed with abrupt brutality.

"Just like that?" muttered Peter, turning to face the house. The rushing blood of fear overflowed in his breast, the ears boomed, his knees were drained. But Garabed broke out in a panicky giggle and scrambled to run; in a flash, the situation was comical. Laughing savagely, they galloped down Henderson Street and up North Street. The houses were still, the tree leaves hung silently in the graying calm, and far off a rooster crowed.

Breathless, they paused before Peter's home.

"One more cigarette," laughed Garabed, "and then I shall go home."

They sat on the porch steps, panting, and lighted up their cigarettes. They both looked up when the first bird uttered a tiny cheep from the branches above.

3

Peter's origins—the more recent ones—betrayed his intellectual convictions. Bent on lolling through the summer, he yet winced inwardly when passing by a group of workmen in the street, and avoided their eyes. His conviction was that history, as a drama, was an unparalleled production—acted by the princes of destiny; directed by that brilliant, envious, and colorless crew that forever sat at the hem of greatness; financed—in terms of blood and labor—by the numberless, nameless masses who paused, only occasionally, to look up from their work and watch; and written by the reality of the hour, the reigning combination of cross-events that was supreme, final, and unalterably history.

His was the role of destiny's prince. Not for him the whispered suggestion in the mad ruler's ear; not for him the weary hand behind the scenes of splendor. Not for him also the plow and the weight of centuries, the stunned, wondrous look peering within the carnage that passes through. For him, Peter Martin—lately of the working class, the Canadian peasantry, and on back to a great-great-great-grandfather who, arriving in arrogance, with casks of Rochambeau, from a barony in Normandy, to forward the cause of the new French empire to the West, saw his fortunes blown up by Wolfe's powder at Quebec and had to be satisfied with a tract of land near Fleur du Loup, which was transformed as the generations progressed from a baronial holding into a region of peasants—grim, muscular farmers—who worked too hard to survive to waste any time on lineage—for him, Peter Martin, the role of prominence on history's stage. For him, then, the splendid leisure and the calm demeanor; the aristocrat of history, plucked from the vine at the right moment, made to burgeon in glory for all to see; he that can wait for his time, blandly assured.

How this prominence was to be achieved he did not know. He only waited, as youth will, for the hour; he only knew he belonged to that great family of the earth whose destiny, whose one responsibility, was to act out a part in history, while the others directed, produced, financed, and stage set, and while supreme reality moved the pen that decided the plot.

And yet, this young aristocrat must drop his eyes when the workingmen glance up from their toil—while they boil black tar in summer's glaze, tear down, build, and repair the setting for the play, whereon the youth will soon perform his regal and tragic part. The prince of destiny is betrayed by the blood of a grandfather who saw fit to kill his own cows; and by a father who believed in work, and rose every morning to lay onto.

Peter passed the workingmen and went on into Galloway. Suburbia at seven o'clock in the morning drifted, meliorated into the outer city; ashcans became more prominent, stood outside the wooden tenements. He passed filling stations and garages, the young sun already at work broiling up gaseous, shimmering fumes. The yellow buses passed. The mill whistles of Galloway called abroad, and it seemed then that the city hastened its pace, answering the call with a vague rummaging sound.

A tenement door opened, slammed. The millworker stopped

to light a cigarette, gripped anew the lunch bag, and then walked briskly toward the red brick mill stacks in the near distance.

Peter walked on. Garabed would be sleeping by now; it would annoy him to know that Peter had not gone to bed, but had launched himself on a sleepy little adventure to the city at morning without him.

But Peter had found it impossible to go to bed. The morning sun, the swift clean smell in the air had called him back to life, called him back for more of the same—which at times held so much wonder that Peter deplored his physical limits. On a morning like this!—to be everywhere, be everyone at the same time, doing everything! To be a Danish businessman in Copenhagen—a brisk, attractive, middle-aged furniture manufacturer—crossing the cobbles at morning.

Or to be an Arabian poet, like Ebn Alrabia, rousing at this very moment in Medina; breakfast, and a brief glance at the scrolls of writing, and a walk to the date grove on top of the hill, attired in those majestic robes and head scarfs.

Or—a deckhand on a ship anchored in Trinidad; the steamy harbor, the sound of the native longshoremen beginning their work. Morning . . .

Peter was very tired, naturally; but so great was his excitement, a slow, sultry feeling stirring against tired nerves and muscles, that he knew he would last out until noon or so before succumbing to home and bed. He planned his morning carefully. First, a bracing strawberry ice cream soda to remove the hot dry all-night taste in his mouth. Later, around ten, a few cold beers at the bar near the Square. Then lunch at the White Star diner, pork chops and Coca-Cola and rhubarb pie à la mode. And during all this, he would watch the people of Galloway, note the color of the sun and sky and the quality of the air among the old dark red buildings downtown, where the sun slanted its rays into law offices and revealed roll top desks, sagging uncarpeted floors, and an occasional cuspidor. Also, he would wander into the five-and-ten-cent stores and see what there was to be seen there, tamper at the toy counter, and perhaps—with grave irony—steal a typewriter ribbon or two.

Peter knew, from past experience, what his sustained mood would be this fine morning. Sleepless, dazed, he would walk around in a sort of fatigue-intoxication, enjoying the subtlest impressions the morning and the city held stored for his mild feeding. By noon, he would be drunk with weariness—perhaps sway a trifle as he walked. Acquaintances would respond to his casual mood and engage him in slightly irrelevant, slightly goofy conversations of his own making.

"Hello there, Socko!"

"Jesus! Martin, you look drunk."

"You don't look so hot yourself." At this point Peter looks over the Square with raised eyebrows.

"Where are you going, you crazy bastard?" Socko asks.

"I'm looking for an honest man."

"You have money to lend?"

"Honest men don't borrow money. They mint it themselves. Did I ever tell you about that?"

"Save it, Martin. I'm a working man. I'm not a college jerk like you. I got to be going. What's the old rose doing in your shirt pocket?"

Peter glances at the rose: "It's a relic, as they say, of the buried past." Here Peter giggles.

"Where did you swipe it?"

"Pick it? I didn't . . . I exhumed it."

Socko shakes his head, slaps Peter on the back: "A few more and you'll be making a speech on the Square. Well I'll be seeing you, you tanked-up track star. By the way, how's prospects for next winter? Think you'll be beating Thompson in the fifty yard dash for dear old B.C.?"

"There is no doubt about it, Socko."

Socko grins with admiration. "Not if you keep this up!"

"A good man," Peter says nonchalantly, "can do everything."

Peter had done this many times before, that is stay up all night long and through morning until noon. It represented, for him, an act of faith he was surprised to find each time it returned. If, with Garabed, he exhibited a cynicism designed to counter-act—or perhaps interact with—that young Armenian's idealism, it only returned to him, in moments like these, as a shallow affec-tation. For the truth was, he loved life and was fond of building it up. Mornings like these, his senses heavy, his thoughts lucid, he found that he could assume a charming attitude to life . . . and he repeated the procedure periodically, like a Christian who goes to church each Sunday to strengthen his belief.

He saw Judge Michael Joyce cross the Square, hatless, a noto-rious political cad with the sun dancing on his graying hair. The sun, the glistening hair removed all doubts in Peter's mind as to the ultimate good nature of life. Morning intoxication dismissed the political and social fact that the judge was the meanest man in town. In a soberer mood, Peter would have watched the judge with contempt and indignation, would have muttered "bastard!" and turned to frown at the rest of the city.

Now he grinned goofily and entered the drugstore to order his strawberry ice cream soda.

Over the straw he considered. Life was good, it was too good to last. Intuitively, he knew this would be one of the happiest summers of his life. The first year at Boston College had been a harrowing commuter's existence—up at the crack of dawn, the bus to the depot, the train to Boston, and then the trolley to Newton Heights and the Gothic pastoral campus. Classes; the smell of liniment in the lockers; the limping clean feel of the athlete after practice; the returning home by trolley, train, and bus.

Now Peter was confronted with three months of summertime leisure. It was going to be good. There were thrilling times ahead, mad happy adventures with Garabed; bucolic lollings with George Breton on ball field, beach, and riverside; ballroom caprices in the sultry nights on the lake; stoic evenings with Dick Sheffield over chessboards, pamphlets, and plans that never materialized; and, most exciting of all, bi-weekly visits to Eleanor the wide-loined, Eleanor the passionate and laughing.

It was, obviously, too good to last. Intuition told Peter that this was the last of his magnificent summers, and all of them had been magnificent. This was the last. Something grave and perhaps terrible was impending, the war maybe, or some violent change in the structure of his Galloway world.

This perfect morning—crystallized in the foamy rose ice cream soda—would also end, and bring the noon. Who was the maker of Peter's noon?

He remembered another perfect morning, when he was twelve years old. It was a Saturday morning in May, no school and cherry blossoms. Aunt Marie had given him Wheaties with cream and sugar for breakfast. A picture of Jimmie Foxx, the baseball slugger, on the back of the Wheaties package. Peter had eaten the cool breakfast in the gladed blue air of morning, had studied the picture of Jimmie Foxx. Outside, the gang—numbering nine to complete the ball team—played catch and bunted and shouted for him to finish his breakfast and come on out: the other team was already on the ball field. Peter, finished, picked up his glove and bat and sallied forth to join his men. They trooped raucously to the field, warmed up, played, and won 26–18—with Peter hitting two homeruns!

A symbolic noon had somehow since intervened. No longer a boy, a homerun hitter, Peter was now a youth—a youth who loved to sit in the Boston Common with his comrade and write bits of verse about the pigeons, the old guns, the monuments and trees and soap box orators.

> *We shall remember this moment*
> *Where that squirrel, bright-eyed*
> *Eager peanut-loving, shall not.*
> *Oh remember!*
> *Frozen sculpture and war machines,*
> *The perishing green of lawn and leaf,*
> *Two souls recumbent on Common ground.*
> *But remember!—*

And now—another noon was approaching. Youth, at some unsuspected moment, would give way to young manhood. That would bring to an end an unbroken series of splendid summers. That would precipitate a ragged shower of bills, summonses, tax estimates; in brief, payment would begin to be exacted. There was a price to bliss, brief summery rose-red morning-cool bliss. It was coming.

Peter finished his soda and lighted a cigarette. He leaned back with what he hoped suggested content and counted the money in his palm: there was a price to the soda too. He paid the bill and walked out. The sun beat down on the Square with nine o'clock intensity. Traffic had grown heavier. He walked.

The coolness still prevailed in the narrow street of old dark red buildings. Here nestled the coolest looking bar in Galloway, with potted palms in the window and an inviting shade within, broken only by the gleaming brass. It was McTigue's; even the name held promise.

Peter passed on, mindful of his morning's schedule. He walked up Center Street, a traffic jam of commerce, lined on each side with clothing and shoe stores, an occasional theater, candy shoppes, and jewelry stores. The sun beat down warmer by the minute; it was the crucial moment of the morning. Peter blinked his heavy eyes and staggered imperceptibly.

He knew now his casual goofiness was gone. Life now pressed for a graver attitude, weather, temperature, the city's mounting activity. Now it was time for the beer. He retraced his steps slowly.

Before entering the bar, he saw fit to gather one last impression from the broken structure of his morning. He glanced up and down the street. The traffic cop in the Square, seen from this side street with his back turned and his arms in motion, seemed either like a conductor presiding over the rhythms of the city or like a madman standing in the sun orating wordlessly. Peter shrugged and was about to enter the shady bar when he saw Eleanor.

She carried her purse at arm's length as she swung toward him, padding on sandal shoes she wore without hosiery. A bandana wound her bobbed hair within.

"There you are!" she sang.

Peter stood tentatively before the bar entrance and blinked a smile. He took in her cool green and white print dress with as much urbanity as he could muster; he noted, with unconcealed admiration, the low cut of the waist that brought out her splendid hips.

"What are you doing at this wee hour of the morning?" she smiled. When she smiled Peter invariably felt a recurrence of their nocturnal excitement. Their eyes met craftily as the traffic rasped unknowing about them.

"I haven't been to bed yet."

Eleanor struck a pose of simulated disapproval. Peter took her arm: "I'll walk you. Whither bound?"

She strolled in stride with his own.

"Shopping."

Peter winced. "No dice—I hate shopping. I'll drop you like a hot potato at the nearest bra shop."

She laughed. Peter's best Boston manner continued to amuse her. It amused him, also.

"Are you on a long drunk?" she inquired. "You look it, you know . . ."

"Why Eleanor, three years ago—" Peter paused. "When I'd met you under the high school clock, blushing. Who would have thought?"

He was tired now; Eleanor lulled him, and to be incoherent with her was to be clever. It was perfect. He felt like talking. She held his arm tightly.

"Who would have thought what?"

"That such a question would arise, I mean ever. I kissed you first in November at a skating pond. You told your diary; I told my intimates. Hell!"

Eleanor laughed. She misunderstood the totality of his thought, as he did; but she heard the ringing hints, and they fitted perfectly into the harmonies of her mind.

"It's a sin to grow up. Periodically you lose your so-called primal innocence. Blah! Now you meet me in front of McTigue's. Soon you will meet me at the prison gates; later at the United States Senate . . . "

Peter shook his head violently, casting away.

"I'm beat out. I need a couple of shots. I started out the morning wooing *la vie*. Later . . . I thought of doom coming. Now I verge on . . . My schedule omitted one fact: the degeneracy of the—What am I?"

"My good for nothin' Joe."

"The degeneracy of the inactive poet. He is so full of ardor. It is only a sign of excess. The other end is at work too. I'm oscillating down toward the other end. It will be worse when noon comes . . . "

Now Eleanor was impatient; he was incoherent.

"The next noon, I mean. What's going to happen? Eleanor . . . ," he had noticed the crisis of her annoyance, " . . . when do I call you next?"

"Monday evening, monsieur?"

"*Si*. Baby of mine. *J'aime tes yeux*."

They laughed at his stupidities, and Eleanor's eyes danced. They were now on Center Street, and stopped in front of a shoe store. She fumbled in her bag.

"This is my first stop. Goodbye?"

Peter nodded and waited casually. She moved off, promising him with her eyes. He retraced his steps.

At the bar, he made rings with his shot glass and then obliterated them sliding his glass back and forth. He ordered a beer and sipped abstractedly. The incoherence of his communications to Eleanor, he now considered, foretasted a madness he would never lose. That Saturday morning in May, and the Wheaties and the two homeruns, all gone. Flaming youth on the Boston Common, the verses proclaiming eternal Hellenic love, not completely gone, but diminishing. (The poet held on to youth until death did him part). Young manliness next, perhaps now; and the insanity of insight and perception.

He thought of Boston College, and the engineering students thereat; and the campus bells. Neurosis did not stalk there. The Irish Catholics stalked there.

The clock said nine-thirty. Later, it said ten-thirty. Peter had drunk six glasses of beer, thinking about his life. With a start, he felt the heat pouring in from the street door. Noon's rapprochement.

And then he knew he was exhausted. Even when his father, Joe Martin, walked in, he knew his last moments had come. The role of destiny's prince, which had thus far justified his morning's dissipation in leisure, now also dropped away, like his stamina. He was pooped and slightly humiliated by his father's workaday entrance.

"Pete!" There was not a hint of disapproval in Martin's greeting. "Having yourself a beer, are you?"

Peter grinned and nodded. Martin chuckled good naturedly and squeezed his son's shoulder.

"Draw me one, Mac," he called. He was having his midmorning thirst-slaker. He buried his lips in the foam and drank as only the old drinker can.

"I just placed a couple of bets," he went on. "I'm taking a flyer on a three horse parlay. Your remember old Devil's Gold . . . we won on him at Suffolk Downs last summer? I've got him in the sixth, across the board . . ."

Peter nodded. Once, he had followed the races with his father, a tempestuous loser, a chuckling winner. Together they had run the gamut of gamblers' emotions: had feasted mightily at the Old Union Oyster House in Boston after a killing at the track, or had ridden home gloomily in the twilight. It was a period in Peter's life, beginning at twelve and vaguely ending now, that had brought him very close to his father. Haunting music tugged at his heart: boy, youth, you're breaking down. He remembered the racetrack, the slanting rose sun at the eighth and final race, his father's face over the program, the hush of the mob in the grandstand presaging not only the running as well as the deciding of the race, but time itself, death itself. The hush rose to a roar, the steeds passed before the tote board, galloped back to be unsaddled, the hush dispersed, the crowd went home scattering a sad refuse of programs, form sheets, tout cards, and torn tickets, the sun set on the scene of blasted hopes, and a graveyard prepared for the night. Peter remembered all this, especially when the grandstands emptied and grew cool and vaulted in the failing light. It represented the melancholy American seriousness. Americans were not sportsmen like the British; they were earnest losers. His father was typical.

He was talking about his bets. Tonight, if he should happen to lose, he would brood in his corner chair.

Peter, exhausted and a bit high, softened up to his old man. Boy, youth, don't break down.

"Why don't we go to the races sometime this summer?" he said.

Martin ordered another beer and grinned. "Sometime in July, when work slacks up. I'll bring me a good roll this time and really take a crack at it. With luck, we'll take in a show and a dinner in Boston . . . " Martin dipped into his beer. "Up long?"

"I got up at nine," Peter lied. "Just met Eleanor a while back. I'm going home in a few minutes. I'm going for a good swim this afternoon . . . "

"Eleanor's a pretty girl. Where's she working now?"

"At Webber's . . . salesgirl."

"Don't swim too much this summer. The coach told me last month it wasn't good for track muscles . . . "

"I know. I take it easy. I'll be training on my own next month. A sprint a day."

"And . . . " chuckled Martin, "take it slow on the beer."

"Don't worry," grinned the son.

"How do you like this little son-of-a-gun!" said Martin to Mc-Tigue behind the bar. "My kid's on a track scholarship at Boston College and here he is slopping it up first thing in the morning!"

McTigue laughed.

"He looks fit enough to stand a few, Joe."

Martin put his arm around his son's shoulder. "You've heard of this boy, haven't you, Mac? Pete Martin."

"Oh . . . *sure!*" said McTigue. "I've seen that name dozens of times on the sports page. I didn't know he was your kid, Joe."

"Why hell yes! Didn't I ever tell you? State low hurdles champ when he was in high school here. B.C.'s ace-in-the-hole for next winter's indoor season. He'll be a sophomore in the Fall . . . "

"Well, well, well."

"Hell yes, that's my boy . . . "

They had another beer, father and son, and left the bar. At the Square they parted, Peter bound for home and bed via the Wild

Street bus, Martin bound for his afternoon's honest work in a quick, short-stepping stride. The sun danced, noon-mad. Peter waited for his bus in a cold sweat of fatigue, no longer a mechanism of impressions; he was now a bag of broken nerves, sagging against the Square clock. Life had wearied him. Enough . . . he was now ready for the sweet death of sleep, for no-expression and no-impression.

He dozed as the yellow bus lurched riverward, a short hysterical nap aberrated with tangents of idea, mists of image. Neurosis stalked through Galloway, a gross black seven-foot monster with obscene wide hips, searching for him. The black hand reached through the kitchen window and snatched up the bowl of Wheaties and cream and the package with the picture of Jimmie Foxx. Garabed shrieked as Peter soared skyward with an evil leer . . .

The bus bumped over the road under repair. Peter awoke nervously and looked at the workingmen boiling black tar in the street; a gust of furnace-like heat blew in through the open windows, and then the bus went on up Wild Street between the trees.

4

There is something about the American home in the suburbs that cures all apprehensions about life. The next afternoon found Peter Martin sitting on his porch with a glass of lemonade, listening to the Red Sox–Detroit game over the portable radio.

Aunt Marie's green Venetian blinds shut out the four o'clock sun on the right and the Quigley elm provided a speckled green shade on the left. Kewpie the cat gazed disinterestedly at the quiet street from his station in front of the screen door. A fly buzzed at Peter's ear and when he fanned it away, causing the hammock to creak at the exertion, Kewpie turned two placid green eyes and stared straight through him, wondering.

Peter liked to listen to ballgames. In the pauses during the announcer's lack of something to say, one could hear the catcalls from the stands and benches, the distant pep-talk of catchers, and someone occasionally whistling. It was a vast and drowsy sound.

"Two and one . . . " the announcer would say. Seconds later, almost as an abstracted afterthought, he would enlarge: "Two balls and one strike . . . " A long silence follows. Someone, perhaps the shortstop, babbles his singsong encouragement to the pitcher. This chant returns again and again, without variation. One can hear the close tinkle of ice cubes as the announcer helps himself to a glass of cold water. Far off, perhaps from the sun bleachers, a voice cries out a long war-whoop. Then someone whistles . . .

"Here it comes," says the announcer. There is a sudden quiet. Thup! into the catcher's mitt.

"Strike two, called strike, two and two."

And again, the vast sleepy comingling of sounds in the hot afternoon sun. The shortstop's weird chant returns, an aeroplane is heard from far off, and the first base coach suddenly hoots to distract the enemy pitcher.

"Bridges is ready . . . here's the pitch."

Tack! The silence is punctuated with this sound and an enthusiastic mass cry is raised. The announcer's voice is almost drowned: " . . . There's a long one . . . out to the left field fence . . . way over . . . " There is confusion. Action has broken out in the hot sun, swift and vicious, dead in earnest. " . . . Cronin is rounding first . . . there's the throw in . . . it's going to be close, very—" The crowd furnishes the emotion of the action going on at second base, the announcer is too rapt to convey what he sees. "He . . . is . . . SAFE! Safe at second, a double . . . " The crowd's long subsiding cheer, which will eventually slide into a sigh and a rummaging of seats regained, begins, as the announcer gathers his wits. "A two-bagger for Skipper Joe Cronin, a long belt off the left field fence . . . "

Ten seconds later, the quiet returns and the monotonous procedure is resumed, the procedure which, during fourteen hundred innings or so in a baseball season, must be carried out slowly, carefully, and perhaps lethargically in one hundred and fifty afternoons of hot sun, infield dust, and white-blinding shirt-sleeved crowds. And throughout the country, broadcast over millions of radio sets, in fire departments (where firemen loll in chairs beside their fire engines, glittering red and rampant in repose, in the long concrete coolness of the garages); in poolrooms where the billiard balls click and the fans whir; in beery, cool, brass-gleaming saloons, where men sit ranged at the bars in complete silence; and on porches in the suburbs, the great and sleepy sound of the baseball game is brought to Americans, the distant whistling, the repeated chant, and the thup of the ball in the catcher's mitt.

Peter liked to listen to ballgames, especially when it was too hot to read or take a walk or go to a movie. He could concentrate on the drama of the game without too much paying of attention, for the thread of the action could always be picked up, after a long soporific sequence, at the instant of the crowd's sudden roar. In the interims, one had time to relax and steal a fancy or two.

It was during one of these drowsy pauses, as Peter finished his lemonade, that Dick Sheffield mounted the front steps and stopped. The sun caught his straw-colored hair and made frizzy wisps of gold.

Peter looked up as Dick was striking a pose intended to convey his contempt.

"The supine pariah," he said, opening the screen door.

"Dick. Come in. What are you doing?"

Dick sat down on the footstool; he never made himself too comfortable, he was always ready to resume his energies.

"How's the desk job?" chided Peter.

"All right, all right, but it won't be long. I'm on to something really hot this time." Dick paused to readjust his position. "The South Sea islands, m'boy. How can you waste your time listening to a ballgame?—you can get the results in the papers . . ."

Peter had lighted a cigarette.

"What are you talking about? . . . the South Sea islands!" Peter said. "Another of your mad plans? Am I coming along on this voyage?"

Dick was half-resentful. "Certainly you are. You just leave it to Uncle Dick . . . follow me and you'll have the greatest adventure of your life. It's simple. We'll be in this war before you can say Jack Robinson. Okay. So you and I enlist in the Army, and when the war comes, boom! we're in the middle of everything. Remember that picture about soldiering in the Philippines, *The Real Glory?*—well, Pete, that's the ticket for us. My brother knows a guy enlisted in the Army last Fall—where is he now? In the tropics, the Philippines m'boy, Manila . . . "

"Sounds swell!" said Peter. "Unless, of course, everything goes haywire, like last Summer when we were supposed to hitch-hike to New Orleans and . . . "

"Different matter, m'boy! We didn't collect the cash amount we had in mind. Economic determinism . . . so we didn't go to Nola. But this is the Army . . . don't cost a cent to join the Army. And—" he raised his hand to silence Peter, who had opened his mouth to speak—"don't bring up other instances!"

"That play we were going to put on in Fordboro . . . "

"I know, money again. We didn't have enough money to put it on, so what? We wrote the script didn't we? Put out the radio or get some music or something. Any cookies in the house?"

"Yeah," grinned Peter.

"Fetch me some. I know Aunt Marie isn't home, I saw her on the Square twenty minutes ago."

They walked into the cool hallway.

"So," said Peter, "you took the first bus up here to get some cookies."

"Partly correct. I also have the afternoon off. Strike at the silk mill. And, by the way, those cookies of hers are good. Did she put a lot of chocolate in them like I told her?" They were in the brightly curtained kitchen.

"Hell, yes," said Peter, opening the breadbox. He took out a dish of cookies wrapped in cellophane paper. "Milk?"

"Ice cold milk? . . . You express my sentiments."

Dick sat on the cool, shiny linoleum and began to eat.

"I wish," he said, "my mother made some of these. Look—" waving a cookie—"this new plan of mine is tops. We want to travel, right? We want adventure, we're sick of this hole in the wall, right? So we join the Army."

Peter was standing by the cupboard drinking milk. He grinned irrepressibly at Dick.

"Who wants to stay in Galloway all his life?" continued Dick. "Didn't we promise each other we'd get around the world some-time? Did we try to go to sea . . . when was it?"

"Five years ago this summer—"

"Okay, and we were too young, they didn't want to ship us out. Unions and all that. Did we try to go to sea five years ago because we wanted to suck our thumbs? No, we wanted the real life. Well, here we are, going on to twenty, still at home, still in Galloway, the furthest we've gone south is New Haven, the fur-thest north a hike to the lower White Mountains, the furthest east is Boston, and the furthest west—Vermont! What a couple of slobs we turned out to be! Here I am wasting my time in a silk mill office, with my feet on the desk all day long—and you! Mak-ing a Joe College out of yourself so you can sell insurance after you graduate . . . "

Peter shouted, laughing, "Insurance! Man, that's no ambition of mine."

"It all amounts to the same, you'll see." Dick got up to get some more cookies and then regained his seat on the floor. "We're flops, both of us. I'm ashamed. We used to say we'd go to Hollywood someday, write, act, anything they want . . . why hell, do you think these people will want us now, we've seen nothing, have been no-where, have not lived and loved Polynesian maids, nothing!"

"Okay Goethe, don't lose your temper."

"Not Goethe, m'boy. Sheffield. Now listen, you and I go to Boston via the thumb next week and see about enlisting in the United States Army, huh?"

Peter shrugged, regaining a seriousness he never could attain while Dick was launched on one of his long monologues.

"I dunno, Dickie."

Dick got up and washed his empty glass in the white sink.

"I'd be game to do anything for the summer, you know that," went on Peter in a considering, preoccupied tone. "The sum-mer represents a time-off period from what you might call my career . . . huh! I dunno . . . After that, I must return to the scholar-ship duties, track, studies, and everything else. I do hate that place! I mean, college itself . . . "

"Of course you do," provided Dick, replacing the cookies in the breadbox. "College is no place for a guy like you and me. You surrender all your greatest talents there."

"To what?"

"Why, hell, to that system of concessions called society."

"You've been reading John Dewey."

Dick moved off down the hall: "It's fact. What the hell good is life if you don't live it to the bone? Jack London was a great liver, Halliburton, even Herodotus . . . there was a man! To hell with college! Did I ever advise you to go to college?"

Peter grinned.

"No," said Dick. "You let circumstances drag you along. Be like Hamlet . . . baffle circumstances."

They sat on the hammock.

"My father would split a blood vessel," Peter said, "if I left college. He's banking all his hopes on me after Wesley took off. He wants me to go places."

Dick opened his mouth in contempt.

"Go places!" he echoed. "And is it you going places? Not you . . . Wesley! I was reading *Lawrence of Arabia* this morning in my office. Why, hell—"

"You're a hopeless romantic," broke in Peter.

"So?" Dick asked, pausing for effect. "The romantics have more on the ball than the others. Those who laugh at the romantics are just jealous bank clerks and unsuccessful writers who become critics. A romantic is a realist who digs in and lives so that he can learn more about everything. Who really knows more about realism than the romantic? Will they ask you that question at Boston College, heh?"

"Pertinence, wisdom, Dick, and allied virtues."

"Sure! I'm your uncle, just stick close on and you'll learn all about it. You haven't learned a thing since you went to college. I was going to phone you the other night and tell you."

Diane Martin came up the street with a high school classmate. Peter watched them, two girls carrying books, walking beneath the richly leaved trees in attitudes of complete insouciance, oblivious to everything but Galloway and its school-world, dates and dances and a new outfit for Easter.

"The Philippines, Pete," Dick was saying. "Just the ticket, and I got it straight from my brother. He's in California and he knows what's brewing . . . the Japanese are hot for war. It's a natural chance for us."

Peter shook his head slowly, a gesture he used whenever he was made conscious of the mysterious contradictions in life. His sister Diane, and her world; and Dick, who had always thirsted for the fantastic and dangerous. A girl whose main concerns were so incomprehensible to Peter, and yet so easy to define, that he sometimes thought all women were essentially like Diane and that he would always know and recognize, yet never understand, the ways of women. And here, Dick sat thinking about things, and hungering after things, that Diane would never understand and—because of that—would never accept as part of the design of life, while Dick could only ignore her and her world in the fury of his imagination and creative energy, and if made cognizant of hers, the smalltown girl's world, could only scoff and carry on with his concerns.

Diane and her companion mounted the porch steps and swung open the screen door. Dick looked up briefly and called a greeting typical of his well-rounded dash.

"The ladies have arrived . . . hiya Diane!"

"Hello, Richard," said Diane gravely, ignoring his gallantry while the other girl giggled and turned her head away. "How's Annie?"

"Swell," Dick smiled.

And with that, Diane went into the house followed by her bashful classmate.

"All you have to do is make up your mind," Dick was now saying. "I know how it is. Your decision concerns more than mine did. With you, it's 'shall I leave college and join the Army?' With me, it's just 'shall I join the Army?' By the way, I'll be over Sunday night for that odd game of chess. You owe me two bucks and a half!"

Peter nodded, watching Dick.

"If the strike lasts all week, I'll be over some night and we'll go swimming at the Brook, maybe Garabed the mad poet will come, huh?"

"He will; he's always wandering around nearby."

"Well," said Dick. "As they say in the cowboy pictures when the villain leaves the honest rancher's house, think it over!" He laughed and got up, swinging the hammock back and forth to rock Peter. "I'm a bad influence. Look out for me. Remember the time I egged you on to go on that chicken coop roof during the flood and we almost didn't get off when it started floating down the rapids?"

"Do I!"

Dick went to the door and stepped out onto the porch.

"I'll walk you down to the bus," Peter said. "And as for you being a bad influence, who was it started you on an alcoholic career? I was the first one to get you drunk . . . remember that quart of Calvert's?"

Dick grimaced. "Not for me. I keep myself in shape for the future . . . "

They walked down North Street toward the bus stop. The sun had by now lost its afternoon fury; heavy clustered leaves overhead seemed to sigh with gentle relief, hung in green profusion waiting for an ebbing of the heat and sunfire.

Dick and Peter stood at the bus stop. Dick had produced his thick wallet and was examining a piece of paper.

"I have a prospect here, Pete, that might come in handy—

should we decide to hold off the Army for a month or two. It's a good paying job . . . "

"What kind of work?"

"The best! Laboring in the sun. That French contractor from Riverside has the contract. Building a wire fence around the Portsmouth Navy Yard in New Hampshire—just near Kittery, Maine. I could get the old Buick in shape and drive up every morning—at least forty bucks a week. How would you like that? Good for you, m'boy, get hard as nails and brown to a crisp."

"Sounds good."

"Here comes the bus. Well, Pete, I'll drop over maybe this week again. Think everything out."

"You know," Pete said, "your family should never have moved away from North Street. Up there in West Galloway the only thing they do is go to church. We never see each other anymore—remember when I'd call you every night after supper? Those were the days . . . "

Dick put his hand to his mouth and called their secret cry, a single yodel. The bus pulled up and yawned open its doors and Dick dashed in. He paid his fare and hastened to the back of the bus, where he stuck his head out of the window and yodeled again, waving goodbye. The bus growled cityward.

Peter grinned. Dick was the kind who cared very little what strangers thought of him or his antics. Occasionally, he still displayed the braggadocio and swagger of his boyhood. Now, Peter imagined, Dick was settling himself in his seat, and toward those in the bus who were watching him with the ironic detachment of the spectator to emotional excitement, he was more than likely directing a frank and good-natured glance.

Such was Dick, nodded Peter to himself as he returned up the street. Nervous, energetic, he still threw his hand up convulsively when someone made a motion with his own hand, as though Dick were yet a boy given to warding off blows, imaginary or otherwise, a gesture he had developed while a member of the North Street gang. There was a boyish quality he would never lose, the swagger in his walk, the way he might tilt his hat if he bothered to wear one, and the nervous hand darting up to ward off the blows that were no longer intended.

Dick Sheffield was the "outline" type. He occupied many of his hours outlining projects that were destined never to come about, he drew diagrams, and as was the case when a boy, he made maps of projected journeys. It was not that he was a failure, that his "plans" became rather a series of abortive attempts; it was only that he apportioned too much to himself, that his vast congeries of projects fallen-through presented a bizarre picture of one man trying to live one hundred lives.

The truth was, Dick had done more quantitative living than any youth in town. A small percentage of his vast program served up a nonetheless huge and varied activity. He had, in the midst of earning his keep at home by working at jobs no other would have dreamed of, assistant radio mechanic at the radio station when he knew very little about radio, and currently a silk inspector at the silk mills in downtown Galloway when he really knew nothing about silk—another youth from his quarter and caste would have applied at the silk mills in the capacity of a common workman—he had, during these highly specialized occupations, contrived to try almost everything the town offered. For the Actor's Guild, he had written several short scripts and played supporting parts, in what he termed a preliminary to Hollywood; he had voyaged to Boston the previous summer with Garabed

Tourian and convinced the Dean of the small college which Garabed attended—Greenleaf College, mainly concerned with dramatics and the arts—that he splendidly filled the requirements for a scholarship, and, when the Dean had written encouragingly later in the summer, marking the triumph of Dick's brilliant personality, Dick had by then launched himself on new projects and completely ignored the scholarship offer. For several months, bewildered theatergoers at the National Theater—Galloway's cheapest cinema, frequented by children and old tramps—were set through the paces of a gaudy, awkward Amateur Show by a certain tall, blond, and smiling young master of ceremonies, name of Richard Reynolds (Dick's first two names). Later, at the Paramount Theater, Galloway's best, Richard Reynolds Sheffield presided backstage among the settings and props for the annual Devon Association show—although, to Peter's knowledge, Dick knew very little about these things, certainly much less than the stage man from Boston who had supervised the backstage work every other year previous since 1932.

Among other things, Dick had, with a West Galloway comrade, painted a huge swastika on the cotton mill's smokestack in 1940 that had reached the front page of the *Galloway Star* and created wild speculation in the city for weeks thereafter. Police were still investigating the case long after the workmen had erased the paint . . .

Peter resumed his seat on the porch hammock and listened to the closing moments of the baseball game. The air had imperceptibly cooled, there was stillness on North Street presaging the suppertime bustle.

Dick's visit had aggravated some lurking doubts in Peter's total makeup. He knew now that he was about to undergo a long re-examination of his life's direction. It was inevitable; small things pointed in the wrong directions, events commingled not smoothly but rasped.

Yesterday, for instance, in the bar with his father, Peter had felt no small resentment at the talk of his future as a Boston College track athlete. Actually, what were those things to one who read *Faust* with envy in his heart; to one who answered, word for word, with Hamlet, the indignities, hypocrisies, and challenges of life in Elsinore a thousand years ago. Track star, indeed!

Dick's stirring taunts added salt to an opening wound—a wound in the curriculum of circumstance. An indignity, to be driven ahead, like an ox, by the stick wielded in the name of "make-some-thing-of-yourself." Make what? "Go places!"—indeed, what places, if not Arcady. "Be a success." Was that not the phrase common to those who would never achieve inward success, who, because they could not come to terms with themselves on spiritual and moral grounds, had to cloak themselves in social garb, so as not to be complete failures, in most cases, in fact, so as to seem supremely victorious?

But here, Peter detected signs of youthful revolt, something quite dissociated from reason. He readjusted his conceptions and emerged with what seemed the truth of the matter: some people wanted to "go places," wanted what he had just fatuously termed "outward success"; simply, he wanted not to "go places" but to find some way of life that could answer his every exertion, that could react to his kind of activity, which, though he had no idea as yet as to the nature of this exertion and activity he accounted to himself, would certainly offer richer and more honest rewards than the way of life opening up before him like some portal to Limbo.

Yes, this would not do. Limbo was the word, a place where souls yearned at a vacuum. He, Peter Martin, who loved the things of the mind and soul, attended a college—certainly no worse than any other American college—which countenanced only mathematics and metaphysics for the mind, and the Roman Catholic church for the soul.

Inward success he desired and—as youth will—he saw no reason for admitting that inward success could only be won at the expense of outward success. Both were within reach, both were available, as far as he could see. Why not?

Now he pondered Dick's proposal. He felt a stirring of the intestines, and, since he had read somewhere that the Chinese consider the intestinal tract the seat of creative excitement, he knew that Dick's were creative proposals. He knew that without having to refer to the Chinese. Dick was a living artist, that is, he was a master at the art of living. His constant cheerfulness, maintained despite an intelligence comparable to that of some who sorrow their "knowing too much," indicated he had, by some Mephistophelean ruse, triumphed over cynicism and doom sense, and was thus prepared to accept life and to undertake its living with quite gay charm.

Or was Dick just a sappy smalltown kid who thought the world was anybody's oyster? His proposal to Peter to throw college out of the window and join the Army was a good and a creative idea, filled with a million subtle promises . . . or so perhaps it was for Dick alone.

For now Peter beheld, in his mind's eye, the enormous complexity involved in what had at first seemed a simple decision. The question Dick had posed, "Shall you leave college and join the Army?" now assumed a dozen interweaving phases.

Peter smiled in his bewilderment. What would his father say? And Aunt Marie? What would it be like to leave home at last and plunge into the regimen of the Army, where one lost the right to exercise his own prerogative? Would America enter the war? And if so, how would he, a dreamer, a ponderer, become a killer and a soldier? And if not war, for how long would the peacetime Army charter his service? A number of years? And if so, how many years would he spend away from a pattern of living he needed—the pattern of study and preparation for a career vaguely leaning toward letters—which he had fashioned by studying for a scholarship at Boston College while still in high school.

His life, he now realized, had so far been simple. It was an astonishing thought for one who had lately considered himself vastly complex.

The complexity had only found play within him. In the actual sense, his life in the last few years had been only as purposeful and humble as the life of the young bank clerk who works year in and year out and awaits periodical promotions. The bank clerk sought next a promotion to Assistant Chief Teller; Peter sought next to rise to the status of sophomore, and gain a foothold on the varsity track team. Where was the difference?

It was the same plodding, cheerless ratiocination.

Peter was depressed. He went into the house and upstairs to fall on the bed. Those questions, and many more, overwhelmed him: he knew they led to other questions of a more abstract nature, questions culminating at the general "why?" philosophers ask of life.

It was hot in the bedroom, the sun pierced through the oven atmosphere with a shaft of sharper, fiery heat, and the breeze was like a warm breath. Peter took off his light shirt and flung it away.

He was angry. It was time to stop thinking, to hurl off encumbering preconsiderations, to wallow in action. Maybe Dick was right, but right or not, this was no time to think about anything, no decisions, no mulling.

Tonight, after dusk, coolness would steal into the air. Especially in South Galloway, where lived Helen O'Day, in that house by the Concord River where yet the oars of Thoreau haunted the summer night. This was the last of the splendid summers for Peter. Very well, then, no time for self-torture and doubt and the stirring deep premonitions of change . . . Time for joy and insouciance! Time for Helen O'Day, and time enough for Eleanor; time for anything and everything . . .

Aunt Marie was home. The suppertime bustle had begun downstairs. Peter roused himself.

In the kitchen, Aunt Marie was pattying up hamburger while Diane peeled the potatoes. Peter drank a glass of water.

"I'm hungry," he said.

"What have you been doing all afternoon?"

"Nothing . . . I listened to the ballgame. Dick Sheffield was here . . . "

"Here," said Diane, "put these potatoes on the fire. I've got to make a phone call."

Peter stood by as Aunt Marie applied a match to the gas flumes. She said, "I got some nice fat strawberries at Bingham's . . . "

"Short cake!" smiled Peter, setting the potatoes on the stove.

"What's Dickie doing this summer?" she inquired.

"He's working in the silk mill office. But he told me he's thinking of joining the Army . . . "

Aunt Marie peered suspiciously at her nephew and paused over the stove. "Army!" she said. "What's he up to now? That child is as crazy as a loon. Always doing the most unexpected things . . ."

"He might not, you know," grinned Peter.

Aunt Marie shook her head and compressed her lips. "Peter, don't you dare listen to him. He's always getting himself into trouble. Did he? . . ."

"No," grinned Peter, taunting her. "No. Did I say I was going with him?"

"You didn't say you weren't!"

Peter chuckled.

"Did he try to put any ideas in your head?"

"No," said Peter, stamping his foot. "Didn't I tell you?—it was just an idea he has. I didn't say I was going with him."

Aunt Marie was still suspicious. "Doesn't that child realize we might be in that war sooner or later? Now what would he do in the Army if war came—what would he do?"

"Fight," grinned Peter.

"Doesn't he know what might happen?" she went on, ignoring Peter's remark. "What kind of fool child is that? Running off at a dangerous time like this! What does his poor mother think?"

"She doesn't know . . ."

"You're right, she doesn't know what fool ideas run through his head. Now you listen to me, Peter Martin, I don't want you to take that boy seriously! All his life he's been getting himself into messes . . . like that time he ran away with his little brother and the police had to search the woods for days . . ."

Peter laughed: "He was going up the river in a rowboat. They were doing alright . . . Dick knows how to take care of himself."

"Peter," said Aunt Marie in a tone suggesting the termination of the subject, "you've no time to listen to any of Richard's crazy ideas. You've got your work to do, a little studying this summer and keeping yourself in trim for athletics. Dick Sheffield has no other thing in the world to do but hatch up his crazy plans. *You've* got your college career to worry about. Do you hear me?"

"Yes, yes," Peter was saying as he retreated to the front room. "Don't worry about it. I know what I'm doing."

He sat in the chair and scowled toward the kitchen.

"I know what I'm doing." Then, in a low mutter: "No need to talk to me as if I were a child. Leave me be!"

Aunt Marie was still talking about it in the kitchen, but Peter shut off his hearing and concentrated on the newspaper. "Do you hear me?" he mimicked savagely. "I've got judgment of my own," he announced beneath his breath, hissing huffily. "Doesn't anyone around here respect my judgment? Goddamnit, I'm no kid anymore. If I want to talk to Dick Sheffield, I'll talk with him all week. That's all! Even if I should want to join the Army with him, by Christ I would! Now then!"

He returned his attention to the newspaper and read the *Galloway Star*'s editorial on the Russo-German front: " . . . the monsters have turned on each other. Within three weeks, it is highly probable that the monster of the Wehrmacht shall have consumed the monster of the Red Army. Moscow is expected to fall in a week, Smolensk is besieged on all sides. When this short but terrible war is over, what will the world be faced with? With the collapse of Russia, Germany will hold Europe in its grasp, marking England's gravest hour since Dunkerque. America across the waters can only hope for the best. The world is waiting in suspense . . . "

Joe Martin walked into the front room and threw his coat

and tie on the sofa. He tuned feverishly on the radio for the race results.

"Got a couple o' bets at Narragansett," he mumbled.

Diane had finished an interminable phone call with one of her school friends. Supper was ready.

"Joe, Peter," called Aunt Marie from the kitchen. As usual, with supper ready, Martin was scribbling with a pencil, his ear cocked to the radio; and Peter read avidly news about Broadway's latest plays in a syndicated column.

As was the custom, Aunt Marie called a second time, adding "your food'll get cold!" to which father and son grunted in reply, but did not budge an inch. The final act came: Aunt Marie stood in the doorway and yelled. Father and son looked up with stupefaction and finally roused themselves.

5

"This Beaverbrook, *Lord* Beaverbrook!" growled Martin over his supper. "*Who* the hell does he think he is, coming around here and trying to get this country in the war! What goddamned nerve!"

"Oh eat your supper and shut up," Aunt Marie said.

Martin pointed his fork at Peter: "Now you listen to this. The last time England asked us to pull them out of one of their European messes, we were suckers enough to fall for it—not, mind you, that America isn't the kind of country that will begrudge a favor. But listen! England is a bully, the sun never sets on what she's stolen. When she bullies some other country and this country strikes back, England turns and runs to us for help. But does she ask for our help? Does she do it humbly? No, she insults us, tells us it's a privilege to help her, sends men like Beaverbrook to sneer and snicker in our midst, make insulting speeches. Look at his picture in the paper! Did you ever see such a goddamned smugfaced Johnny Bull in your life?"

Diane, gravely listening to her father up to this point, now remarked, "Miss Walton told us today in Modern History class that England attacked the Boers because they wouldn't give up their independence . . . from 1899 to 1901 it was."

Martin laid his glass of lemonade down with a bang.

"You're telling me?!" he cried. "My own poor father used to talk about nothing else all day long. I was about Peter's age myself, but

I had no education and spent all of my time working twelve hours a day in the cotton mills . . . "

Peter was annoyed. "Stick to your point."

"My father knew what was going on there in South Africa . . . maybe the only man in Galloway in 1899 who had his eye and his mind on world events. And he knew what the English were about, he knew them for what they were. He was a young man when the English slaughtered all those poor Egyptian niggers in the Sudan. My father *hated* the English! And I don't blame him one bit!"

"Imperialism will go out soon, so don't worry about it," said Peter, grinning into his glass.

"Oh you think so! The British Empire is still there, isn't it? They have their greedy fingers in India, in our own poor Canada, in the East in China and Singapore, all over to hell and gone, in Africa, everywhere! Now they're in trouble again—naturally—so they throw up a smokescreen and come over here smelling around. They'll get us in trouble before they're finished . . . " Martin sighed at the inevitable. "And then we'll have war again. It's always the people, the masses who get it in the neck in the long run."

"Well, don't you think ever of the English people, the English masses?"

"They get it in the neck too."

The argument was ended. Martin and his son always agreed when politics, affairs of state, and the "pith and moment" of great world events were boiled down to the suffering, the dogged stage-building of the masses of the world, the father with sadness, the son knowingly.

"*Le pauvre peuple,*" sighed Martin, relapsing into the French of his father. *"C'est toujours le pauvre peuple à la fin du compte, et puis ça cera toujours la même pauvre vielle histoire . . . toujours le peuple. Ah misère . . ."*

And here, oddly enough, Aunt Marie nodded in abeyance with her brother. Some old kinship between them emerged, as always on the occasion of Martin's return to his family's tongue, a kinship lost and strange in the world of the present. This scene had the same effect on Peter, each time it was re-enacted by his parents, as that when word of Wesley, his own brother, was spoken . . . a strange mystical feeling that returned like the memory of old, old songs, or the sight of an ancient family photograph cast in the old brown daguerreotyped world of the past.

Peter left the supper table and went up to his room in a semi-trance.

"Le pauvre people," he mumbled, shaking his head in imitation of his father. *"Ah misère . . ."*

He sat in his easy chair and for the first time in months lit his old pipe. Twisting around, he gazed out the window at the neighborhood. The trees rippled quietly as the sun ebbed, spreading a redder glow; a regiment of clouds, colored blue, orange, and white, migrated slowly toward the sun. Far off, on the river, a motorboat growled placidly.

"Ah misère . . ." Peter sighed. His father, perhaps, was nobody's fool. Politically misinformed, yes . . . but that was the lot of the workingman in this or any preceding age, to be wrong about politics. The workingman produced; the politician did something else . . . *he* was a tyrant, or else he spent his time enjoying the fruits of his office. But the workingman just produced. And then wars came, the politicians declared them and the workingmen fought them. Why? *"La même pauvre vielle histoire . . ."*

There was a wisdom to all this, its deep sense of irony exclusively his father's, perhaps unmistakably Gallic altogether. The shaking of the head. What a subject for a painting! . . . a workingman shaking his head, or better, an old French peasant with the years seamed on his face, shaking his head, and adding to this a gesture Martin often used, holding the shoulders up in a lethargic shrug, all of this indicating a deep old knowledge preserved in the French race—the knowledge of Voltaire, of Molière and Balzac, the joyous reveling in this knowledge, of Rabelais—that the people, always the poor masses, lose out in the end.

Here was a lesson for Garabed, by God. But Garabed would have his answer ready. The Gallic shrug? The irony of the French? What of the French Revolution and the Paris Commune? What of this and what of that? The Great Liberal Movement moves on! Even the French know that! Why, Pete, the French are the most democratic and vital people in the world! Fall of France be damned! Look at Leclerc's fighting French Army, mustering together in Africa. De Gaulle's in London. Look at the French underground! What of all that? . . .

No room here, in the scheme of Garabed's logic, his and the whole contemporary world's logic, so vital and energetic, so progressive and aggressive, for the old French peasant with the seamed face shaking his head and shrugging, and saying: *"C'est toujours le pauvre peuple à la fin du compte . . ." Always, when all is said and done, it is the people.*

Peter got up and leaned against the wall, and looked at the quiet street below. His room had darkened. The sun had grown huge and bleary red, a breeze touched off the shaking of tree leaves, and soon it would be summertime dusk. Voices below rose softly in the air as soft. A tender shroud was being lowered on this life. With the darkness, and with the smell and feel of it, would come the old sounds of the suburban American summer's night—the tinkle of soft drinks, the squeaking of hammocks, the screened-in voices on dark porches, the radio's staccato enthusiasm, a dog barking, a boy's special nighttime cry, and the cool swishing song of the trees: a music sweeter than anything else in the world, a music that can be seen—profusely green, leaf on leaf atremble—and a music that can be smelled, clover fresh, somehow sharp, and supremely rich.

PART II

SKETCHES AND REFLECTIONS

While sailing to Liverpool as a merchant sailor in 1943, Kerouac consumed John Galsworthy's *Forsyte Saga*, which stimulated his own interest in composing a multivolume saga of novels. Impelled by Galsworthy's achievement, Kerouac returned to New York committed to plotting the events and characters of an always-evolving literary universe across a sequence or series of books. As is clear from planning documents such as "For *The Haunted Life:* The Odyssey of Peter Martin" and "For *The Haunted Life*," Kerouac was intent on expanding his tale of the Martin family, as first set down in 1942's *The Sea Is My Brother*, into such a multivolume saga. The following selection of sketches and reflections document his early efforts at the saga model as they unfolded across the decade—efforts that culminated in the composition of the initial draft of *The Town and the City*, completed in 1948.

Kerouac's planning documents for *The Haunted Life* identify war as a primary catalyst of sociohistorical change. In the case of World War II, Kerouac attributed the inevitability of such change to the "great cross-migration" of an entire generation into the theaters of war, onto military bases, and into the centers of wartime production. A case can certainly be made that Kerouac's interest in nomadic activity as a powerful agent of personal transformation was rooted in these reflections on the migrations of the war years. Moreover, his understanding of the war as a catalyst of modernity may partially explain his abandonment of literary realism and naturalism upon his completion of *The Town and the City*. In the closing pages of that novel, Kerouac portrays Peter hitchhiking the nation's highways in a black leather jacket, gesturing toward a new aesthetics of mobility and speed that would be more fully realized in *On the Road*.

The surviving planning documents for *The Haunted Life* are followed in this section by "Post-Fatalism," an early metaphysical and cosmological tract in which the young Kerouac valorizes individual determination against the overwhelming will of the universe and human civilization. In that document's final sentence, he imagines Wesley Martin as romantically embroiled within these timeless human struggles. "Typing Exercise" finds Kerouac brooding over his intentions for *Galloway*, another early entry in the Martin family saga—a saga the aspiring writer has come to see as a test of his creative will. As such, this document provides a glimpse into the young author's insecurities, as he expresses his doubts as to whether the subject he has chosen—life in Lowell, Massachusetts—will be too "provincial" to interest his fellow Americans. In this same document, Kerouac makes a passing but significant reference to Allen Ginsberg, and it is during this very same period that Kerouac's work first brings the coalescing world of the New York Beat writers into literary focus. That world serves as the basis for "The Dream, The Conversation, and the Deed" (with Lucien Carr cast as Kenneth) and "There's No Use Denying It" (with Ginsberg and William

Burroughs cast as Bleistein and Dennison), as Kerouac begins sketching the urban milieu that features so prominently in *The Town and the City*. Both sketches display the influence of Kafka and Céline, and stand in stark contrast to the drowsy Galloway depicted in *The Haunted Life*.

"There's No Use Denying It" features an antiliberal rant of sorts, foreshadowing the animus toward city life that Kerouac further expounds upon within the *Town and the City* documents that round out this section. Despite his qualms regarding provincial Lowell as spelled out in "Typing Exercise," Kerouac evidently finished *The Town and the City* highly suspicious of the "intellectual decadence" he had encountered among his friends in the "City-Centers of America." These early concerns anticipate Kerouac's public dismissal of the New Left (including Ginsberg himself) years in advance of its actual emergence as a coherent political movement.

T. F. T.

For The Haunted Life:
The Odyssey of Peter Martin (1943)

War can make evident the phenomena of change more crush-
ingly conclusive than can ordinary times. That is why war, in itself, offers the richest possibilities in any literature. Dostoevsky's
terrible and depressing novels have nothing to do with war, but
one flinches at the thought of what he might have written had
there been war in his novels: think of the ordeals of Raskolnikov,
and add war to them.

The novel need not be the unhappiest expression in art. I do
not seek to achieve a consummation of sorrow—not deliberately,
for the sake of eliciting a meretricious "power." But whereas war
trebles the sorrows of men, and whereas war is with us, the novel
must move accordingly.

Before the war, young Peter Martin was of course not conscious of great and sorrowful change. Perhaps because, primarily, he was too young and had not lived long enough to witness
change. Had he lived through a time of peace, change would
have stamped his heart with sorrow nonetheless; but because he
lived through a time of war, the change crushed him completely.
This is yet another facet of the haunted life. (The others thus far
discussed: the wandering which war enforces, especially great
global wars like World War I and World War II; the phenomena of human personalities first drifting then disappearing into

the sprawling panorama of life (and war life); and the peculiarly haunted life of a personality like Peter Martin, who knows many people and journeys to many cities and lands, and wonders.) (To this one may add the loneliness of the sea, and of ports, which induces a sort of semitrance on the wandering seafarer.)

Peter Martin is shown, at the beginning of the book, as an average American youth in an average and beautiful American town. There are the great trees of summer, the hot afternoons of baseball, the swimming, the thrilling Autumns with football and riotous October (melancholy old October). All this is of course taken for granted and thoroughly enjoyed. Peter's uncle no less is of course taken for granted and thoroughly enjoyed. Peter's uncle no less complains: things aren't the way they were when *he* was young: this is Peter's first contact with the fear-of-changing motif. He scoffs at the uncle, who launches off on lyrical reminiscences of the "old days"—the circus in 1898, the coming of the hated immigrants, and so forth. He scoffs, the youth, but it takes only three years of war and change to make of him a youthful carbon copy of the melancholy old man! The "old days," indeed, becomes one of Peter's phrases. He does not allow the egocentric change-sense his uncle indulges in to warp his thinking, however. He realizes as Wolfe did that you can't go home again: he realizes that no one can, and that the famous phrase can be repeated forever, and could have been uttered by a Babylonian of the days of Cyrus. He realizes, from this cautious and intelligent conclusion, that the fires of new life spring from the ashes of the old: It means enough to him to induce efforts on his part to make a new life, of his own shaping. The world he was given (the summer trees, the high school, the sports, the lemonade on the circus grounds) was a good world, but it faded, as all worlds do, and faded rapidly, as they do in war: and now he must make one of his own.

The Haunted Life will be a very sad book. It can't be otherwise: youth is shocked by maturity, but war adds to this shock enough to kill youth forever and create a generation of old young men, the sad young-old men of F. S. Fitzgerald and E. Hemingway. How war can kill more numbers than are found on the casualty lists! How terrible and sorrowful and great with emotions of breaking pain! Peter does not die a thousand deaths in his loneliness and wandering and battle with violent death and yearning for peace: he breaks! He breaks, as a voice will break, or as a heart will shatter, or as a brain may snap. He breaks apart, like a smashed old clock. He has not the will nor the life to gather up his broken remains. He verges on insanity, he is terribly sensitive to things of this sort. There is no hope for him. The death of his brother Wesley, though far and impersonal, provides enough loss and irony to assuage a Lear; the spectacle of his broken brother Slim, booming with pain on a waterfront street, asking [?] is enough to frighten [?] each ideal, each faith, and leave a black vacuum of despair. The woman he loves is not enough: it never seems to do for a man to base all his mind and spirit on the union with woman. Peter seeks more.

The book is divided into three parts. The beginning is beautiful and Americanese, Peter is home, Peter is nonchalantly alive, an eager intelligent youth who reads and discusses, travels and laughs and dangles hearts with lasses. The war comes slowly, at first as a supreme adventure; then as a bore: and finally, as a terrible and lonely and desperate adventure; and the last part of the book is not yet formulated, or is so, only vaguely. It will come with the writing.

The thread of the Odyssey runs back to the beginning and forward to the end, the end which is only a beginning and an interruption or activity presaging more activity, more life. I may safely predict the nature of the end of the book: Peter will be making concrete plans to build a new world of his own, knowing all the while that this will be the lot of his child, and of his children, and get [sic] thereafter that no one can keep the world he was given, but must make one of his own, and prepare others to make their own . . . for the fires of new life spring from the ashes of the old. Change is not a process of disintegration; it is the law of organic life, *growing*. (As for the personality of Peter and its denouement, more anon.)

For The Haunted Life *(April 12, 1944)*

133-01 Crossbay Blvd. Ozone PK. L.I.

War creates a situation synonymous to that of a great cross-migration. People who ordinarily were habitually suited to sedentary lives are quite suddenly wandering the earth. Soldiers are sent to all parts of the world, workingmen migrate to far places in their nation and in some cases to foreign lands, country boys sail stranger seas than did the Ancient Mariner. The virus of the war enters the veins of men, women, and children. Women, who follow their husbands, or join the services, or simply take advantage of the times to take wing, can be found a thousand miles from home, anywhere. Children are only too eager to follow their elders. I have heard of some cases, in chaotic occupied Europe, where children go off in groups and are lost in the sprawling scene of the great wars, great crusades, and the like. It occasions what may be termed a "nomadic decade." What the result of and reaction to, such a decade [will be] can only be determined—in a pattern significant to over-all understanding—in the course of time.

Politically, one can reasonably assume that the people of the world will become more open-minded toward international issues. A small town boy from Vermont who spends three years in England will no doubt, in the future, show a lively and personal interest in that nation. He will have adopted England forever. The sailor born in Chicago who journeys to New Zealand will have his opinions regarding that stout little isle, and can be heard, in 1960, discussing the four Maoris of the House of Representatives. It is not beyond the imagination to predict that some of the marines who took Tarawa will be interested in knowing how the island is to be governed, now that it has become an American mandate, what it will promise, and so on.

Those who went to Italy, to North Africa, Egypt, India, Australia, England, Alaska, and even Greenland and Iceland—by the millions—will have become aware, despite themselves, of the oneness of the earth. The same applies to the Germans who were sent to Scandinavia, Russia, the Balkans, Italy, Africa, to wage war, and to the Italians, Rumanians, and other satellites of Hitler. And think of the hordes of Japanese who would never have seen the East Indies, Burma, India, or China; the South Pacific islands, the Aleutians off Alaska, had it not been for the war. Never, I am certain, in the history of mankind have so many nations seen the mass influx of foreigners within the space of a few years, whether they be invaders or "liberators." Never have so many men travelled throughout the world at the same time and witnessed people and customs and institutions of lands other than their own. These men easily number close to the one hundred million mark. There is no way of computing the number of civilians who were forced to wander, refugees, workmen, and military auxiliaries alike. The whole panorama is staggering in its proportions.

And when one considers the amount of national cross-migration in individual nations hard at war, the uprooting of families from regions where each had been settled for generations before, the situation grows to a proportion like that of a gigantic earth-shaking which scatters men and women helter-skelter, separating families and lovers and friends in all directions with no regard for traditional humanity and dignity. The picture presents a canvas of disrupted roots drifting like tumbleweeds in a thousand crossing winds. It is an enormous canvas. And though it no longer represents traditional humanity and dignity, it is no less humanity and dignity; rooted or adrift, the soul of manhood prevails.

What is interesting to note, with some anticipation, is that when the earth ceases its shaking and scattering, the world of men will attempt to straggle back to a traditional form. Finding this impossible, the wave of mankind—now seething from the after-effects of the tempest—will settle slowly into a new form, man by man, city by city, nation by nation.

What will be this new form? How impetuously shall change have been shocked out of its customary lazy pace! And how haunting will be the memory of those who have lived through the great "cross-migration," the shaking of the earth—for men were not born for this sort of life. They were born for quiet, and the hearth, and the family which takes upon itself a place on earth—a region—and calls it its own. Knowing this, men have nonetheless doomed themselves, by their folly and humanity, to indefinite frustration of their true and final need—the need for home and peace—and will continue to hurl themselves at one another, each time on a larger scale until they learn, through the lesson of great war crusades, the oneness of the earth and the likeness of men. This is for the future to consummate.

Meanwhile, the haunted nomads wander and wage war, and will return to father others like them. The mystery of life is augmented, it deepens, but as I have mentioned, the soul of mankind prevails.

Post-Fatalism (Bastille Day, July 14, 1943)

Once I have explained the vast order of the network of the universe, how can I then rationalize its seemingly blind order? Does it require a Kant to do so?

Indestructible matter reorganized itself to form the universe; time is matter in motion. The reorganization of matter, as it was, seems now to have been done splendidly, considering Newtonian order in the planetary systems and considering the definite rate of growth in organic life as explained by Darwinism. There is order, growth, expansion, even Spencer's progress from homogeneity to heterogeneity. The universe is growing more complicated, thus more subtle. Each achievement of man adds to this matter subtly.

The general will of this universe, which defies accidents, which defies chance, moves on in its moiling, orderly chaos. One entity, one man moves within this changing network; he struggles for triumph, and to the extent that he is willful, he may achieve it, but to do so he must pursue a winding course. There are obstructions everywhere, for this man is not the only entity in the universe, but one of billions. An analogy: matter cannot go through matter, it must top it, circle it, or bowl it over. This man, his own will, and the will and impulse of the universe, determine the man's destiny: it is inviolable, perfect and terribly irrevocable.

History proves what I say. See now if you can change what has gone before. See, too, how this history wrote itself, if not by the moiling will of billions limiting the personal will of one great figure; or, on the other hand, if not [by] this great general will destroying the weak will of an obscure figure. See too how death happens: it is no accident; it is the general intention of the universe, and when it happens, the die is not only cast, but the race is run, the circle is drawn, and all is as it should be, for such is life.

This is not fatalism: it is Post-Fatalism. Before an event may occur, one man may prevent it by exerting his individual will, and if he chooses so, and if he has the strength and vigor and determination. But if the man does not prevent the event, and the event occurs, it is obvious that the man did not change it, nor did the universe shy from bringing it about, and so it occurred, and therefore it was meant to be. It is Fate only after it has happened.

This network, then, what relation has it to us, although we can affect it, and it can affect us? I believe firmly that this network, the combination of the General Impulse of the Universe and the Individual Impulse of a Single Entity, is a guiding force which leads one to one's destiny and is irrevocable, final, and orderly. It guides us, like God, and is perhaps God. It watches over us. It does not protect us, but in guiding us, it watches over us, and we are not so alone, so unrecorded, so unwatched, and so directionless as we think. These two wills, ours and the world's, lead us to glory or to horror: we should not whine over it, because a challenge is a challenge and we should all accept it. In accepting this challenge with force and courage, we are facing life on two feet and are prepared to enjoy the adventure of its infinite possibilities with all the warmth, all the richness, and all the valor inherent in the human breast.

Sit now as you read this by the window, and listen to the sounds stealing into your room from without: it is rhythm and order, the divine rhythm of life. And this is the network within which society strives toward better days, not blindly, but irrevocably, slowly, and majestically. Songs of beauty may go unheard, heroic deaths unsung, beautiful flowers like the Rhodora unseen—by men; but life records them, the universe recognizes them, and the existence of these things, though obscure to men, are necessary to themselves and thus adds to the rich stores of human achievement. We are guided, and nature and the universe believe in us as much as we believe in them. For this reason, we are not alone. Human love can make it doubly certain that we are not alone. Thus I write of Wesley Martin.

Typing Exercise (1944)

Again I find myself at the nadir of doubt concerning that ineluctable weight, *Galloway*. It seems that almost every day I have to convince myself, by some neurotic ruse or other, that the game is worth the candle. Today, I feel that the novel as planned falls far short of those powers I now command: it is merely an introductory piece to more mature work, it is a prelude, an overture to a symphony. Yet the scholastic sounds that have existed in my mind ever since its original conception in 1942 persist. Why?

Is it by force of habit that I continue to return to the structure and idea of *Galloway*? Oh there is an interesting history behind it, its recurrences, its abandonments, its doubtfulness. If one were to take Mr. Allen Ginsberg seriously in his latest opus, *Galloway* is by way of being some sort of haggard thing I have been picking up and laying down for years in the course of neurotic indecisions and anxieties: that and nothing else. Has he ever lived with a work for the better part of three years? Ineluctable weight! He dashes off a "Last Voyage" in a night, and then spends three months revising it: then when you ask him how long it took to compose, he will say "Three months." That is fine: Mr. Ginsberg is a careful artist, three months it is. But I, with my three years, ah that is but neurotic procrastination. Well, no, it has grown *with* me—the first draft, entitled *The Vanity of Duluoz*, is a half-stupid mass of words. The form is there, of course. I revived the book in

1944, two years later, with better success, even if I return to it and find myself doubting its artistic success, even if it were worked out to an incredible degree consistent with the imagined work.

I shall combine Symbolism with Naturalism in *Galloway*—but to take myself at nineteen, and that dreary provincial town, and make a work of art out of it commensurate with the liveliness and *intelligence* I want to achieve, that indeed seems impossible, and a boresome task without even the fruit of my own satisfaction. Poo!

I am bored at the thought of Sebastian and the others. I am bored at the whole picture of it. I can bring to it no enthusiasm. Poo again. But I shall do it, I suppose, although—and this is the crux of my circumspection regarding the whole affair—although I feel that I can master a more mature subject, *now*. I go back to ignorant yesterday, and gad!, do I have to trace the lines that lead to knowledge? That is not my purpose . . . that is not consistent with the doctrine of grasp and growth. I don't lie in bed with my nightcap, because I have no *Paris* to offer! Who wants to bother with Lowell, Mass.? Who, who? unless it is the fool who, by force of habit, perhaps by a compulsive inanity, by a failure to organize recent experience, must give up and start at the beginning, the dreary Paleolithic beginning, and work on like a dog. Fa!

Now I say, let us not get frantic. What a mountain of merde!

The Dream, the Conversation, and the Deed—Some of Peter Martin's Frenzy (c. 1947)

A dream he has in the Brooklyn house prior to waking up that morning: of himself standing in a dark basement of some gloomy almost abandoned house, in the veritable dank cellar of the house, talking in the dark to two other men, one of them his "elder cousin" and the other "an officer" of some sort: and while listening to their conversation he is conscious of a third person in the dank basement with them, who is however in bed, in some dirty bed behind squalid hanging curtains, somewhere near the coal bin of the house, and this person, though not sleeping, is absolutely still, and also, as he gloats there in the dark, it is understood in the dream that he is an IDIOT. Upon awakening from this dream Peter goes into the kitchen for a glass of water, returns to the living room, and sees, with great interest and horror, his own bed in his own dark room behind dark hanging heavy curtains. He is that idiot. He goes back to sleep and dreams that he is in an exalted state, happy, and DOING ANYTHING HE PLEASES IN THE WORLD; simply from sheer idiotic joy, and it seems that he has committed a crime in the course of these feelings, a crime of some sort the consequences of which he isn't even interested in, he has no interest in such things, he is an idiot—yet still guilty, and in the course of the dream, convicted to die in the electric chair. Up till the last moment of his execution in the death chair Peter is exalted and happy, chatting eagerly with everybody and even with his executioners. But when the last minute comes, when the man steps behind the curtains to go and turn on the electric current preparatory to his being sat upon the chair, he freezes and shivers from the awful terror of death—just afraid of death, still not even understanding what he has done that is a crime, though realizing that he has done it.

That same day, in Manhattan, in a conversation with Kenneth: he comes to Kenneth exalted and happy and tells him to come and get drunk with him. Ken says he has commitments, and he is sincere in these claims, Peter believes him, so they drink about six shots apiece in a half hour and Peter rattles on happily. But suddenly Kenneth begins to say he isn't buying 90% of the things Peter is saying, he says Peter has grown "frenetic," foolish, and is no longer the great sincere, reverent Martin. Peter says that someday he'll throw a party in an apartment in New York which will continue for years and years, he himself being there only half the time, and Kenneth says: "Oh no, you'll put aside ten thousand dollars to take care of your mother and father and you'll come around with 55¢ to get drunk on—as always." Peter smiles bashfully and wickedly. He almost tells Kenneth that he knows too much. Kenneth says the thought of him made him sad, and that the worst thing that could happen to him would be any success of some sort, which would put him in the hands of people who would turn his head and heart away from Martin sincerity. That doesn't impress Peter so much, though. But finally Kenneth says, "Don't you realize how really disreputable you are, Pete. You are the most disreputable person in the world. And you don't care.

You don't believe in anything you yourself say. I've never seen such awful guff, AND YOU KNOW IT YOURSELF. And your disreputability is more than just that, it's a horrible way you have of holing-up when you don't have to, it's a coyness, and thank God the reason for the coyness is not coy itself. Your reverence for life is a kind of damned disrespectfulness. Any kind of success for you, Pete, and all I'll do is pray for you, on my knees. I can't buy you anymore. Yet I still like you and love you just like a brother." Peter says that why the hell doesn't Kenneth just get drunk with him and stop picking on him, but Kenneth continues just the same. Peter is abashed, he doesn't understand what Kenneth is saying, he keeps saying "Huh?" "What?"—and Kenneth keeps just simply laughing at him. "What is it that you don't want to hear, Pete?" he says. Peter tells him that he can make him feel abashed but what is the point of that?—and Kenneth insists that his point is not that at all, he only wants to tell him that he's falling down into a terrible pit and is becoming completely dishonorable. The more he piles it on, the more Peter realizes the truth of it all. Peter leaves Kenneth feeling hurt—with only this one consolation: Kenneth won't let Pete go to his girl Jeanne's house for a shot of whiskey because Peter makes her "act silly." Peter assures Kenneth he had never given Jeanne a thought, but just as he says that, he realizes that he's lying bald-facedly. Kenneth knows it: he smiles again. But Kenneth assures Pete that he's not jealous, he doesn't like Jeanne that well (and at this point they both realize that Kenneth is now lying)—but that Jeanne is a problem to him and Peter only aggravates the whole situation. Kenneth says he doesn't "buy" the way Peter "comes on" with Jeanne, which Peter explains had always seemed to him just affability and sociability (another quickly realized lie). Ken is afraid of Pete. It is

Peter's only consolation, since the kind of criticism Ken is laying on him always hurts him. Peter feels low in spite of the consolation. He's certain that Ken's afraid of him. It was the smile on his face that made it worse: Pete couldn't even fathom his own reaction to it at all, or that is, he didn't want to. He was an idiot, he knew, through and through, just as in the dream: he was bound to do some crime soon, from sheer joy, from shrewdness, amiability: an idiot of all sorts.

That very selfsame night, after a lot else has happened, after the suicide of Alfred, when Kenneth leaves town, in the wildness of his feelings, with sudden surges of pure madness, Peter seduces Jeanne—just simply piling one mad thing upon another, hurting everybody in one grand great final gesture, hurting himself, Judie, Jeanne, Kenneth, everybody, with great joy. And the thing that maddens Peter is that he is someone to be feared, someone to be exiled if necessary—it maddens him and at the same time he walks around late that night in ecstasies, ecstasies of triumphant evil, all kinds of things he never "knew he had in him," yet always foresaw. He thinks in these crazy terms: "I'm an idiot, I don't drink from the cup of life, I drink it all up and then I swallow the cup. And I don't care *what* I do, it's a real crime, that's what the dream meant. With me it's not what I do, not WHAT, but HOW MUCH—the more and more and more the better. I would swear on the bible and on my mother's name in Ken's face that I hadn't seduced and been seduced by his girl, I would do it with tears in my eyes, and even as I returned the bible to the other room I wouldn't even grin in the dark. I do things just like that— consciously, only I'm worried about it all the time." In proportion to the wrongness of their deed, Pete and Jeanne make love all the more violently that night, like voluptuaries, madly. Also, when she leaves in the morning, he looks in her desk drawers and reads Kenneth's beautiful false love letters to her. He walks along the streets that day with an astounded ecstatic grin.

At night he gets his mother mad at him and anxious by stating that a married man can always go out and get drunk as much as he wants, married or not . . . saying this with real disrespect. His father has given up trying to talk to him about these things, he doesn't even shake his head as in the old days—he just stares down thinking of his imminent death. Oh the horror of his last days, and Peter there—!

Peter lays down in his room and wonders if he shouldn't stop doing these things, and become good again—like a good little boy. Again he doesn't care. He realizes that some great sorrow will straighten him out, or just his disrespectful decision to go at things differently "sometimes." He just piles up horror after horror upon himself.

Dostoevsky—" . . . An innocent soul, yet one touched with the terrible possibility of corruption, and with that wideness with which a soul still pure consciously entertains vice in his thoughts, nourishes it in his heart, and is caressed by it in his furtive yet wild and audacious dreams—all this naturally connected with his strength, his reason, and even more truthfully, with God."

There's No Use Denying It (1945)

THERE'S NO USE DENYING IT: WHEN YOU HAVEN'T ANY MONEY IT'S EXTREMELY difficult to feel freely indignant about the stupidities of others. When you haven't any money and never had any in your life it's just as plausible to turn on yourself and let loose a series of self-recriminating blasts. But as I rode away from Queens on the subway, spun in my own little cocoon of indignance, as the subway smashed and crashed along towards Manhattan, I forgot all about never having any money, and made faces at the article I was reading. It was one of those wartime things, a "letter from France," in the *New York Times Book Review*, and it was supposed to give American readers an idea of what the French were thinking and writing now that the Germans had been cleared out and chased pell-mell across the Rhine.

The author was a professional imbecile, of the phony Liberal kind that now have American letters monopolized. One of those strangely neo-Puritan people who spend all day thinking about how best [to] achieve the common good of all, but never for a moment realizing that such a thing is impossible while there still exist people like themselves. Because people like themselves only want one thing—like everyone else, naturally. Only a lot of other people aren't making hypocrisy a rallying cry and a profession. It is these professional imbeciles, I said to myself, blue with un-important rage, it is these people who have the press, the radio, the cinema, and letters by the balls. I read on with an increasing desire to be hostile.

Now this phony bastard was trying to tell me that outside of what he had already reviewed—and that, by the way, was a series of dull hack pieces about the heroism of the Resistance and such other completely irrelevant crap—now he was trying to tell me that all else he found on the bookstalls and kiosks was not worth reviewing because it had no "political significance" in it. He mentioned something Pablo Picasso had written, and from what I could gather, Picasso had amused himself with a little allegorical trifle, charming and light, as the saying goes. Our friend the professional journalist and bull-thrower found that absolutely irreverent in view of the great heroic and epic period France had just survived.

I had an urge to spit in the newspaper, but that is the sort of thing that is not done in America unless you're a refugee just off the boat crawling with the verminous hates of Europe and spitting them in a shower of jealousy into the white-tiled kitchens of Ozone Park. So I just folded the paper and jammed it inside a handle of the sliding doors, and gave myself over to a session of scowling.

I was thinking that for God's sake literature should be the last form of expression we have, uncontaminated by this new form of high pressure all-out professional and official Phonyism. I was thinking that sometimes you could find a book—maybe something by John O'Hara on this side or by Julian Green on the other side—and could relax in a limitless sea of natural and unconstrained saying. Not always coming up against a wall of generalities and radio lyrics. Radio lyrics, you know, cover a lot of ground: they serve to assure us that the bumpy road of life sometimes leads, if we have courage, to a bed of roses. All the way from that to glorifying our already half-hammered-in idea that the Germans are much meaner than we could ever get to be, because we have raised our children to believe in massaging their gums before brushing their teeth, like we elders do, and to believe that God is on our side because we water our lawns, trim our hedges, keep the garage clean, fuss around the workshop behind the kitchen, and go to church on Sundays where the priest assures us that we are united against religious intolerance, the undemocratic way of life, and something called aggression. Across my mind flashes all the symbols of the radio lyric, if you want to call it that. I saw Philadelphia gentlemen drinking whiskey in a paneled room, sometimes over stamp collections or chessboards, other times, by God, over blueprints. I saw pretty young things rushing into a soda fountain. I saw their fathers reclining in a beach chair on the lawn, with a glass of beer and something like the *Saturday Evening Post.* I saw their mothers mixing batter in the aforementioned white-tiled Ozone Park kitchen. I saw young boys eating cereal and getting healthy right before your very eyes. And whenever I saw a soldier, he was either on furlough, rushing into a soda fountain, or reclining on a beach chair on the lawn, or eating the freshly made cake in the white-tiled kitchen, but never, mind you, drinking whiskey. Or I saw the soldier lying in a foxhole thinking about all the above things except the whiskey, covered over with a three-day beard, and taking a bead with his rifle on some grinning monkey of a Jap. I saw all these things and realized how amazed I would be if I ever actually saw them in the flesh.

Not always coming against a wall of generalities like that. That's what I wished. And all the time I was thinking these things, having my little round brooding gripe, I realized that I had some friends in Manhattan who never even bothered to read the *New York Times Book Review*. I thought of them laughing at my unimportant little angers. To them, all this nonsense was something to be expected. They were shrewder than me, that's certain. They even probably thought of making hay while the sun shone. What did they care? They had long ago learned that hypocrisy pays. And that's what they wanted, these smiling friends of mine, they wanted to get paid.

But someday, I resolved, I would vent my opinions to them, and let them laugh. At least I would have made my position clear.

What angered me the most was what one of them, Bleistein, had to say about my view of things. He said that I was burning myself out getting fierce over questions that were already passé. He called me a Romantic. To Bleistein, a Romantic is a neurotic. Personally, he, Bleistein, didn't mind hypocrisy; as a matter of fact, I was certain that he thrived on it, and washed in a big bathtub of it. I could see him splashing about happily in the dirty water with everybody else, happy as long as there remained for him the opportunity to feel someone's leg.

Then I had another friend, by the name of Bill Dennison, who not exactly liked to wash in the dirty water, but preferred to sit somewhere nearby, in a beach chair maybe with a mint julep, or a pipeful of opium, and watch the fun. He annoyed me most of all.

As for me, with all my hatred for the dirty bath, there I was in the middle of it trying to get out. This amused Bill Dennison to no end. Everything amused him.

I got off the subway at Radio City and got up on the street. It was about seven o'clock in the morning. A fine May morning, with the little Sixth Avenue trees all arrayed in new leaves and everybody walking around in the sun. Some of them doubtlessly on their way to murder and robbery, but nevertheless, they were happy to be out in the May sun. Even the Broadway Sams I passed on my way to the Polyclinic Hospital, those so-called Runyon characters who linger about on the corner of 50th street and Broadway, even they looked happy. They stood around counting their money, as usual, but this morning they were doing it with a certain zest and delight. It's really frightening to realize that these sallow-faced monsters, with their perpetual expression of pouting and pained anxiety, faces like crumpled, sagging old dollar bills, even in the younger ones, are human. For then you realize that you are brother to a monster, and a possible monster yourself.

I walked west towards Eighth Avenue. There were some more Broadway Sams on that corner, the Madison Square Garden variety who bet on the prize fights and basketball games, and even on the circus trapeze acrobats, I strongly suspect.

The Polyclinic Hospital is between Eighth and Ninth Avenues. It is the most miserable hospital I have ever seen. It is a hospital for the poor, that's why. The floor cleaners are all Bowery bums who drink bay rum mixed with cheap wine. In the wards, you see sickness and smell sickness and become sick yourself. There are some good doctors, there, however; but of course, I know nothing about medicine. It always stands to reason that hospitals like these are, by some sort of slow biological process, bound to become miserable, in spite of the original condition and atmosphere of the place, because the poor, and particularly, the sick poor, seem to love to breathe out misery in a way that eventually lends that misery to everything around them. Like the British working class of the 1930's who used their new bathtubs for coal bins.

As I got off the elevator on the fourth floor, sure enough, in front of my eyes, was the sick poor, and more miserable a crew I have never seen. These people were sitting on benches in a hall-way waiting to be given some sort of electrical shock for their deafness, partial or otherwise. The living symbol of the sick poor was there, vividly and sickeningly, in the form of a woman and her young daughter. These two were dressed in what is popu-larly recognized to be the garb of the refugee, the woman with her cumbersome shoes and thick cotton stockings and the little girl with a silly shawl. I watched them with disgust, sitting as I was, directly across the hallway from them. They both wore a mooning expression that seemed to whine for pity. Both of them had large dark eyes and long faces and they didn't seem to know where to put their hands. It must not be said, however, that they felt out of place. They were right in their element, and there was even a kind of little impertinence in the way they ignored the sensation they were creating in me. I watched them unceasingly. Still they sat there, drooping with misery, resigned, as they say, to a wretched pathetic fate. They did not move, they completely ignored their companions in ear trouble who sat all about talking and gesticulating. I would have sat there all the rest of the morn-ing watching them if Alexander hadn't happened to see me from the fire escape.

He switched down the hall towards me, with that splendid unconcern of the aristocrat. It's amazing how little democracy there really is, in America or anywhere else. I thought Alexander would walk over their heads.

"Joe, why don't you come out on the fire escape," he cried, lumbering around their benches.

"Where's everybody?"

"We're the first ones."

I got up and followed Alexander out to the fire escape, first turning to see what the old woman and her daughter would think about that. They had both turned their mooning faces in my direction. There was a certain amount of awe in their expressions, as though going out on the fire escape were something beyond their rights. Which is just what they wanted to think, I'm sure. People like that wash in a dirty bath, too; they just love misery, more and more of it, and the dirtier the better. You can do no worse than relieve them of their misery, for then they won't be properly allowed to moon around.

The first thing I wanted to do was tell Alexander what I had been thinking about on the subway. He was clever enough to see through hypocrisy, of course, but I suspect that he went me one better, and was clever enough again not to bother about it. In any event, he started to talk before I did, and the more he talked, the less I desired to tell him about the damnable little "letter from France" that had so incensed me. Because John Alexander is a subtle young man. He was one of Bleistein's "moderns" who went beyond the passé and concerned themselves with the new problems. And the new problems were all subtle. In this realm, hypocrisy, as a matter of fact, had little meaning. A psychoanalyst did not accuse you of hypocrisy when you withheld psychic facts and information; he only saw that there was strong resistance in your subconscious. Well, I was young enough to wade into new ponds, confusedly, of course, but happily.

Alexander was clearly upset over some dreams he'd been having. It was funny to see him being upset. This big adolescent hulk, with the dreamy Casanova eyes, the perfect profile, the good family, the buxom intelligent mistress, the good clothes and well fed look, and the sophisticated, semi-effeminate manners, was being upset. You saw him bubble with surprise when the latest homosexual scandal came out, or when it was learned that a certain Gotham society matron had given so much to so-and-so. The rest of the time he sat around with his mistress cooing about jewelry or women's hats, about sex or a clever line in Henry James. Now he was all upset about his dreams.

He had a boyish laugh that crinkled up his eyes gaily. It was also a loud laugh that burst out of his enormous body and rumbled around. "I was so upset, Joe, I had to leave Joan's and go get a room in William Hall . . . "

"Why on earth?"

"I don't know! I just couldn't stand it. I was frightened by the hallway there. *Don't* you think it's interesting!"

"I certainly do," I said frankly. "What the hell were your dreams about?"

"About women's hats!" he roared. "It's the damnedest thing. It seems as though I were sitting on a roof next to a lot of other roofs, all different in size. And then again it seems that these roofs were only women's hats. Joan thinks I was sitting in a cradle."

"That's possible."

"If so, Joe old boy, I'm sure it must be the remembrance of something that happened long ago, had something to do with women's hats and one of mother's long-forgotten teas."

"Maybe some old matron came up and gave it a diddle, hey John?"

"Or maybe she wanted to throw me out of the window. *Gad* knows!"

He was shimmying all over with laughter. He let out a long sigh and giggled a bit. "I was *so* upset! And Joan is all worried about it now. She's all for calling in a psychoanalyst immediately."

"Especially if you insist on being chased away from her by these . . . by these inconvenient nightmares."

Always when I was with Alexander, I spent all my energy trying to contrive wry and humorous remarks. But it never worked out. The remarks always came out lame. And he was so good at it. I'm sure I bored him.

"Where *is* that Hosker!" John said, with some annoyance, glancing at his wristwatch.

"Late as usual," I said, to fill the gap.

"When these people get out we'll have some room to sit." John was referring to the sick, poor, and deaf. They were slowly disappearing, as the electrical shocks were being meted out full tilt now in the antechamber and the line was thinning. To John they were something that filled up seats, these people. To me too, for all I know. When there's a crowd in your way you always think of machine guns. I've mowed down my share on Times Square.

Hosker now came prancing around the corner of the corridor, clacking his heels smartly, with that trail of cigarette smoke that always followed his vigorous movements around.

"Hup! Hup!" he yelled up the hallway, seeing us on the fire escape. He rushed up to see if we were smoking. "Won't be long now, boys. Where the hell are the girls?"

John and I followed Hosker back into the hall. The last of the ear patients was just leaving, a big man with handle-bar mustaches who was always cupping an enormous hand to his ear. He turned around and grinned at us, cupping his ear. I filled the void by yelling, "So long, Pop!"

He nodded vigorously and went.

"You boys didn't smoke did you?" Hosker said.

"Had my last one yesterday morning," I lied.

"Where *are* these people!" John exclaimed painfully. "I've got to do some shopping this afternoon."

We were waiting for the other kids who were in on this racket with us. Every once in a while, about twice a week, Hosker had us up there for throat tests. He had a kind of colorescent machine that made readings on the relative inflammation of your throat after smoking so many cigarettes. Hosker was connected with a certain cigarette company; he was a chemical engineer, and had himself invented the fantastic gadget inside. The whole idea of the tests, which fortunately dragged on for months, was to prove that his company's brand of cigarettes had less inflammatory effect on one's throat than other brands. It was all scientific, you see. We were not supposed to smoke for twelve hours previous to the tests. After the first reading, we were all given cigarettes and told to smoke like hell, which we did. We all smoked different brands. We all sat around smoking, talking, while Hosker rushed around making his readings, for a few hours at a visit, and for that we all got five dollars. Hosker was our happy, vigorous, goodnatured little gold mine. He was really a very nice person. This is proven by the fact that after a while, the kids just simply called him "Hosker" and even made cracks about his invention. Hosker took it all, as I have shown, with a great good nature. On top of that, Hosker had a good job and he didn't give a damn one way or the other. These men always prove to be the best. They bear no ill-feelings of the kind that come out and bite you.

Around the corner now swept the good Dr. Schoenfeldt. He gave these tests a dash of medical legitimacy. Hosker was supposed to be Schoenfeldt's assistant, but you could tell right away that Hosker knew more about it. I suppose Schoenfeldt had been hired by the cigarette company just for his name and prestige, and as I say, to give the tests, the experiments, that needed professional sanction. Schoenfeldt was a distinguished looking German refugee doctor. He knew something about Hosker's colorescent machine, of course, and about everything else that went with the tests of course. But in the matter of these tests, I had the feeling that he should have acted more like Hosker's assistant than anything else. Hosker had invented the thing, and when it broke down, he repaired it himself. At any rate, they were both good fellows, and we were getting our five dollars a throw.

It was one of the most pleasant jobs I ever had. I should say, *the* most pleasant.

Schoenfeldt sailed into the antechamber to hang up his coat and curtly inquired, with a thick German accent, where the other guinea pigs were. Hosker lit up a cigarette and tapped his foot. "These girls are always late!" he said. "Come on, Paimpol," he said to me, "get on your white horse and go and get the girls."

The only thing I could reply was, "Gladly, if you get me the white horse." One good remark deserves another.

Hosker went into the room where the throat machine was and started to fuss around. Dr. Schoenfeldt went into the office and called up his wife. John and I sat waiting, and I was mad for a cigarette. I poked John and put two fingers up to my lips, which is a signal meaning you want to smoke. He shrugged and we went out again on the fire escape.

There I lit a cigarette and took three long puffs, sharing them with my companion. I inhaled so deeply that the smoke was still coming out of me when we went back to the hall bench.

"Goddamnit," I said, stretching out my legs, "let's get going."

It was hilarious the way we all complained at this little job, as though we were stokers demanding better working conditions in the fire room.

John was still ruminating over his dreams, and now he giggled. "God, but if these dreams go on, I'll go mad, really Joe. Those hats! those damned hats! I wonder if there's anything homosexual in there somewhere . . . "

"Certain kinds of hats can be called phallic symbols."

"And then you know, my mother and I, in this other dream, were in a cafeteria. I ordered, of all things, sausage and spaghetti. But before I should eat the spaghetti, I want the sauce cleaned off it in a sort of spaghetti-cleaning machine. Sausages! Phallic symbols! don't you think?" He giggled uncontrollably. "And that spaghetti business, oh God!" When John said "Oh God" you could hear it all over, echoing back and forth. "Some sort of fallopian symbol there. Fresh from the womb, the spaghetti must be cleaned of its tomato sauce."

"Charming dish," I said, pleased with myself. John was really upset about these dreams, but I couldn't be of any use to him in the way of sympathetic understanding or whatever you will. Conversely, I was certain he would not respond to my preoccupations with hypocrisy. And already I could feel my hostile interest fading. In another hour, I would be ranting about something else. We are all mad.

"I don't know," said John brightly, "what mother would say to all this, I really don't. Gad!"

Hosker came out and sat with us. He had a newspaper in his hand and started to read it nervously.

Outline of Subsequent Synopsis:
The Town and the City *(1948)*

After BOOK ONE: "THE TOWN AND SOME OF ITS APPUR-
TENANCES" and the introduction to the members of the family
and their world, in BOOK TWO: "AN AMERICAN SPRING-
TIME" we find more about the life of the Martin family in the
Town, set in a truly American Springtime landscape, however
with the beginning of events leading to the several interconnected
themes of the novel, these being: the American family and how
it can disintegrate, what this can lead to and what it significantly
means in American culture: our life in pre-war, war and post-war
times: the deep meanings of town-feeling and city-feeling in this
country, their antipodal moods: the transplantation of European
"culture" within our own, by outcasts and malcontents, as a kind
of revenge for failure within the fold and as a means of individual salvation, and the danger of this special kind of decadence to
our indigenous vigor and organic health: and all the misty hints,
meanings, evocations, longings and unknowables of an unex-
pressed culture—the whole catalogue of American things and
tones that have only begun to be expressed by spiritually American writers like Fitzgerald and O'Hara and Wolfe, and denied by
Americans like T. S. Eliot and Henry Miller and the psychoanalytical writers who apparently believe that "culture" is an exclusively
foreign phenomena.

In this section are scenes exploring more of our own culture and at the same time the active plot gets underway towards its revealing conclusions. The Martin father and little Mickey spend a big day together at the races and restaurants and theaters in Boston, and this sets forth the awe and wonder of the little boy in juxtaposition to the dignity and love of the old man; there are scenes showing Elizabeth Martin forlorn and lovesick in the April rain, the strange boy she loves (Buster Fredericks) who wants nothing more than his "horn" so he can play the blues and some-day become a great jazz musician, and scenes of their romance in the lonely and savage places that they go to on his ecstatic motorcycle, the music in their hearts; there are scenes with Peter Martin and his friends, ballroom dancing on the lake, baseball games, swimming, and one wild drunken trip to Vermont, all-night talkfests—all of it setting the stage for the pathos of the fact that almost half of these boys get killed in the future war; and Joe Martin settles down in Galloway starting a gas station, dividing his time between work and sports and romancing in the typical way that American youngsters have; young Charley works in Joe's gas station; there are scenes showing little Mickey's neighborhood activities, his "gang" and their doings, and also the elaborately imaginative private life he leads in his room with all kinds of games he invents; there are Saturday nights in May when Mrs. Martin is home alone with her cousin, whence they tell each other's fortunes in tealeaves and smoke Fatimas, and the Spring moon shines down through the trees around the house and all the night is soft and rich; the father bowls with his friends, plays the horses, plays cards, neglects his business and loses money; there are scenes about Ruth Martin and her dates around the town and the young set she moves in; and meanwhile there's Francis Martin's job in Boston, and the futile hesitating love he has for a beautiful college girl that ends with his hating himself even more, his lonely wanderings around Boston, the bitterness and hatred for his lot always seething. Through all this, running like threads, is the fact that Mr. Martin is seriously neglecting his business like a man who is undergoing a second restlessness, and moreover he does not heed his wife's admonitions; and secondly, the reckless Elizabeth passionately presses the issue with her beloved and persuades him to elope with her in the near future, although she has yet to finish high school.

In BOOK THREE: "A CRISIS IN THE FAMILY" the Martin father loses his business and declares bankruptcy, and Elizabeth elopes with the young musician Fredericks. But these are only the externals of a deep inner crisis in the family. Concerning the father's folly and neglect, no sides are taken in the household on the issue, the whole family retaining a cohesive natural loyalty in the face of any adversity. Here I wish to show that the average American family is not ugly and torn by neurotic strife as can be so easily supposed from reading a lot of the current sensational literature: the naiveté of the American is the source of his great strength. Now the family has to move out of the old Martin house, which is a great American tragedy in itself, and move to a flat in Merrimacville situated among tenements. This affects the kids in so many ways. It makes it easier for Elizabeth to make her rash elopement: she and her young husband migrate to Hartford, Conn., which at the time is a booming war-plant town, and there they get jobs in the defense plants and young Fredericks plays his saxophone at night in the cabarets: the whole world of jitterbugs is introduced, in a mood of "blues in the night" that existed at the time all over the country. (This is carried through to its present

1946 development: I find that jazz is a great subject to explore.) Meanwhile Peter Martin is struck hard by the family crisis: he broods the whole night long on the eve of his departure for the sophomore year at college, where he is expected to become one of the great halfbacks in recent years: homesick and melancholy, however, he suddenly leaves college after only two weeks, roams the South in a dreamy daze, and finally returns to Galloway, helpless yet angry. He wants to work and help the family, and gets a job in Hartford also, where he spends two months of strange joy and loneliness—the product of feeling for the first time in his life the inherent purge of failure. Alexander Panos remains a devoted and doting comrade. Peter then comes back to Galloway and gets a job as a sports writer on the Galloway newspaper, where bitterness, anger, longing and ambition rage in his soul: he is revising his whole idea of life: there is always something appealing about a young American working on a newspaper and finding the harsher lineaments of his world-around in the pursuance of his job, always something dark and brooding, angry and passionate. Meanwhile, Pearl Harbor has come and everything is even more confusing. Young Joe wants to enlist right away but he has to choose between going off to war and helping the family, and temporarily chooses the latter.

Meanwhile, the Martin father, having made animosities in Galloway due to the well-known excess of his temper, finds that he has to work in out-of-town printing plants. He begins at this point a long stretch of loneliness and labor in cheap hotel rooms away from home, and it is here that he begins to fail in health and in spirit, which ultimately kills him: so many disappointments follow his having lost the Galloway business: Elizabeth's elopement, Peter's abandonment of a brilliant college career, the war, the plight of the family, and so on to more and more pain, defeat and regret.

Rose and Ruth get war jobs. But understandably enough, it is little Mickey who is hit hardest by all this: there are scenes full of pathos depicting his confusion and wistfulness, how he misses his old neighborhood chums, and sometimes trudges across the town with his bat and glove to play with the old gang but they have already begun to forget him. As for young Charley, he's just waiting to come of age so he can join the Marines, and meanwhile he works at odd jobs.

In BOOK FOUR: "WARTIMES" we get the strange and brooding life that occurred in America during the war. Peter joins the merchant marine and travels all over strange seas, there are many returns to his land, he is drunk with the power and mystery of Arctic mountains and African coasts, there is sadness and strangeness and longing, and the great train scenes in the U.S.A. with all the soldiers and sailors and young wives, the quality of nighttime and loneliness and loss that the war produced in the generation, the songs of the time, the reunions and partings everywhere, the atmosphere of farewell and night rain glistening in far-off places. Joe joins the Air Corps, and there is the beginning of his love affair with a girl from the West: he is assigned to service in England, and there are the scenes there, particularly one heart-wrenching reunion with Peter in blacked-out London. Francis is eventually drafted, for his part, and almost immediately put under observation in a psychoneurotic ward: scenes here are of utmost importance and pathos, inasmuch as they reveal one of the great aspects of the war, the inability of some to stomach the regimens of war and the resulting pathetic confusion of youngsters who thought they were insane. For Francis it is just further proof that he is the only sane man in a mad world. His father visits him in the ward, and Peter on another occasion. The gloomy madness of Francis is given free rein. The doctors realize that although Francis is not mad, he is indeed unfit for almost any of the responsibilities of life, but Francis scorns their judgment. He is finally discharged and he goes to New York City to live alone and work, where his wan spirit at last finds its true home. There is the mother with her anxieties and fears and the letters she writes— (wartime letters offer a vista of feeling)—and her loneliness. Ruth goes off to join the WAC, where she eventually meets her future husband, a softspoken Southern boy, and there are scenes of their courtship and marriage just before he goes overseas to end up on Okinawa, and always the train rides, the partings and reunions and the feelings of farewell everywhere . . . The Martin father continues to work out of town, and his bitterness against the war and his own life grows, he wanders, an old man now, alone and living in cheap hotels and working all night long in the printing plants. Little Mickey meanwhile applies himself to his schoolwork with absorbed devotion and his inherent ambitiousness begins to show. Young Charley enlists in the Marines and goes off to Quantico for training, and there is a scene where he meets Peter in Washington just before going overseas, whence he and his brother spend a melancholy night sitting up in the park across from the White House among all the other kid-soldiers sleeping in the grass, a scene of youthful desolation and waste as the warm lights burn in the White House windows . . . (Charley never comes back from Tarawa, and Peter is the last of the Martins ever to see him.)

The Martin mother, in a desperate attempt to reunite the family, moves to New York City, to Brooklyn, where the old man joins her and they both go to work in the city. Little Mickey finds himself suddenly in the clamoring streets of the City, confused and frightened, and in the public schools of Brooklyn. The other boys come home sometimes, Peter (who has taken to living with a girl between sea trips, with a wild bunch of young war kids), or Francis occasionally for Sunday dinners, or Joe on one furlough, Ruth the WAC comes home on a furlough, and Rose (who is now a nurse)—there are gay Christmases and joviality, but always nonetheless there is the quality of something gone and lost, of farewell, a feeling that everything is farewell, with the great wartime scenes in America and overseas, and all the things that happened, the drinking and desperation of the time among the young, the loneliness of the older people, night and farewell and desolate rain, and the letters that people wrote . . .

Peter receives word that Alexander Panos is killed in Italy, and in his great sadness, he journeys to Asheville, the home of Thomas Wolfe, where he and Alexander were going to go together after the war . . . And there is Peter in the Smoky Mountain night waiting for the ghosts of Alexander, of Thomas Wolfe, of a lost American vision, of all the lost Americans in the war . . . And the train along the river near Asheville howls as it did for Wolfe so long ago.

In BOOK FIVE: "THE CITY" we come at last to the grand meanings of high civilization and city-feeling and the specific impact of this upon the Martin family. How the family struggles through the maze of enigmas, conflicts and fatal complexities of city life, through all that tension and skepticism which has come into New York and several other great American city-centers and which is alien to the deep pulse of life in the town-America, how the family emerges strong—this is the expression of a true optimism for American mankind, based on the facts of American life and grounded on the nature and substance of the life here. There is no purpose in pessimism save death, no goal in carping criticism save destruction and no end in hatred of this country and this way of life save the abyss. I believe the American is a plain man and his goal is simplicity. The American culture is still so young that it hasn't smoothed out the rough edges of its shape yet, we still have "minorities" and we still have decadent outcast groups and individuals from the "majority" or the "mob," we still have the actual infiltration of alien political ideologies, and much confusion and conflict—but the thing will take shape, and the time has come particularly for American writers to stop apologizing to European culture for being Americans and to proceed within the full Springtime of a new culture and society. This is "Americanism," but "Americanism" down past the political surface of the term, down to the deep roots of an actual national feeling that can't be denied, down to the domain of America's "unuttered tongue."

Now, in this book five, there comes over Peter Martin the spiritual apathy and desolation of city-feeling, in this particular case in the realms of "intellectualism" and "emancipation" that find so much approval in city-centers of thought. Peter with a loving heart seeks "enlightenment"—and like everyone else pursuing that course in an unfinished culture only ends up with the decadent Existentialism of European culture. How Peter, running the gamut of all this to spiritual anarchy and sophisticated spoofery and even drug-taking, and to that last stop of the European soul: psychoanalytical cognition: how he finds himself finally wishing to die under the crushing weight of excessive pessimism. One of his decadent friends commits a murder, in which Peter is involved, and in that sequence the full flower *du mal* of a Baudelairean city is dramatically shown, with all the gloomy ends of the night, the evil and the perversion, the brutality and the Roman squalor shown for all it is worth. (This material is contained in the Phillip Tourian murder novel.) And there are hoodlums, dope addicts, petty gangsters, marijuana pads and scenes in fantastic Lower East Side hovels and hideouts along the waterfront that give to Peter at last the realization that the city is a cruel illusion . . . No longer does the Brooklyn Bridge soar to freedom for him, for now he's lived under its dirty belly and seen it reach greedily across the sky for Brooklyn—and he has known Brooklyn too, known it well. The despair that comes over Peter is almost final: he begins to feel the need to retrace his soul back to earlier meanings, he thrashes about the city like a wounded animal . . . And meanwhile Francis is involved in that gloomy decadence of his own, he indulges in literary diatribes against American culture in the little chi-chi publications of the city, frequents sophisticated cliques around the city and announces that he is "waiting for the atom bomb to drop" and all that stuff. He is preparing himself for a blind-alley life of bitterness and incalculable disbelief—for a spiritual suicide. And Elizabeth Martin, after spending a few years of her marriage with Fredericks in war plants all over the U.S.A., and after their inevitable and violent separation, now turns to a wild reckless life of Dionysian excess, operating along the edges of the jazz world (she has become a topflight vocalist) and drugs and higher prostitution along Broadway . . . yet always filled with loss and longing for the life she had known in Galloway. This is actually what the City has done to three of the Martins . . .

But the rest of the family, as by an inner necessity, clings unconsciously to the spiritual strength of American culture. Now that young Charley is dead, little Mickey—almost sixteen years old—begins to make a brilliant mark in school and prepares to enter a prep school on a scholastic and athletic scholarship, just as Peter had done years before. In the clamor of Brooklyn Mickey has grown into a quiet and resourceful lad nevertheless, almost as though Charley's death had transferred his greatness to him, and we also see that unlike Peter, Mickey is never going to know excessive doubt and experiment because of this atmosphere he has chosen for himself—that domain of science and technique which continues to open up in America. Mickey is going to become an engineer. Meanwhile, the father's health fails, largely due to his hatred of the city and his loneliness for the old way of life of New England—for to him, the whole country is falling to pieces as he sees some of his children go down under so tragically while the others have to struggle so gamely: little Charley's death on Tarawa, Joe's subsequent injuries in Europe, the havoc of war on his faith and soul, the wretched downfalls of Peter, Francis and Elizabeth in their real despair, and that phenomenal rise of "leftism" and Marxist sympathy in America during the war, especially in the pressure-group areas of the city all around him—all this convinces the angry sick old man of the fall of his beloved America. He sits alone at home in Brooklyn while Mickey is in school, the mother is working and Peter is wandering fruitlessly about the streets—and he weeps and mutters and prays and shouts out his anger. The doctor now gives Mr. Martin less than a year to live: he has a form of cancer . . . For Peter to witness the slow death of his once mighty father is the culmination of despair.

Meanwhile Ruth's young Southern husband returns from Okinawa wounded, and they start their life together slowly (the war is over now), meeting all the heavy post-war problems with which all such young veteran couples were confronted in 1945. They can't find a place to live, the boy is weary, prices are high and wages are low in the South and all those things. And Rose, meanwhile, is married and living in New England. This had reduced the size and strength of the Martin family, and the old man is dying . . .

But Joe Martin is coming home from overseas, and after a brief passionate re-courtship of his girl, during which he is torn with jealousy and wracked by all the confusions of the returning veteran, he marries the girl, brings her home with him to Brooklyn and sets out to hold the family together—for Joe unconsciously believes in the family and always will.

And this is when the father dies.

In BOOK SIX: "DEATH AND RESURRECTION" the focal scene, the climax of the story, is the funeral of the Martin father in his old hometown of Lacoshua in New Hampshire. Here all the members of the family are brought together again, the wandering sheep and the faithful and the black sheep too, the despairing and the courageous, to the scene of their original land . . . the land of the Town . . .

And in those scenes the whole mood and trend of the novel is seen in an illuminated flash. What do these kids think as they see their father in his coffin and remember the years of life in New England, the war, the City behind them? What is it that they feel? What do they say to each other? What occurs to their souls when they see the old man lowered back into the land in the old cemetery?

They find themselves again in the old landscape of the true American life, after wars and cities and confusions and madness, they see their father in the coffin and they remember everything—

each in his own way . . . And it is Peter who is overcome with the greatest emotion of his young life, who sees everything at last in the purifying light of love and devotion, who realizes the deep meanings of life and love and courage and death. It seems to him as he sees his father laying there in the coffin with his ink-stained hands folded before his grave reposeful face of death that a great and gentle demonstration of life's one supreme meaning is being made for him—for here is his father, surrounded by his sons and daughters and the wife of his life, and the beloved old friends and relatives of his New England land, in old New Hampshire, in the brooding hill night, all this after the bitter years of Brooklyn's clangorous air, of illness and anger and longing—here is his father's realization of an ambition, back home again and at last with his kind and kin and in his true land, but now he is dead, he is dead, after so many years of suffering and loneliness and longing, and it seems suddenly to Peter as he stands before the coffin weeping, that all the richness to which his father's longing soul had been dedicated, an American richness, now returned to him after he is dead, when he can no longer know it, is a richness of longing—that in the life of such a man, despair is cast aside because the heart wishes to love and to long for life—and Peter realizes that he too must become a patriarch in this life, he too must strive and be filled with longing and love, in the face of anything and everything. He sees now that life in the world of all his fathers, in America, is infinite longing and courage and simplicity—and he sees that he, Peter, must cast aside the doubts and pessimisms of the City, and return to his father's land and life . . . Elizabeth Martin is also overwhelmed with repentance as she sees her old father in the coffin. She makes up her mind then and there to come home, and start her life over again . . . But Francis stands in gloomy silence in a dark corner and says nothing. The little widow, Mrs. Martin, is surrounded by three great sons now—Joe, Peter and Mickey. The family is going to come back to life—it is death and resurrection . . .

After the funeral, Peter slowly becomes a new person, returns to the old American self he had in the earlier part of the novel, but fortified now with a youthful kind of wisdom and strong friendships and new hope. He is fortified by the example of his great brother Joe and warned by the example of his brother Francis, and he, Peter, the Alyosha of the Brothers Martin, takes over the mood of the finale, for he's the central figure in the whole unfolding meaning of the story, he is the uniter of all the varieties of human and American possibility in the family, and he goes forth at last a true and a *believing* American.

Here the essential awe and wonder and delight of American life reasserts itself in the last pages of the book, with all the overtones of glee and boyish gravity that exist in the culture, and in the resurrection that comes over a country after a war and over the lives of people after a death, we find Peter the uniter visiting all the scenes of this Resurrection—Joe's new home and new family in New England, where the old brown and gold of American joy begins again; a football game in which Mickey Martin stars and is the toast of his comrades; he visits Ruth and her husband in the South, understanding their hopes and meanings and feeling again the mighty surge of American vitality running through his blood because of all these things; he plans for his life and career and future patriarchy; he travels West and sees the vista of America broadening before him . . . and he remembers, he remembers—his father, Alexander the lost boy, the girl he had loved in the city which had broken their love, his brother Charley, his dead comrades, he remembers everything and grows stronger within the surge of true American strength (which is not to be found in the City). For he has come to see that "hell is the inability to love"—that the joys and sorrows of life are the necessary shadings of a courageous soul—that man is a cultural animal capable of saintliness and character, and not a "brain" of overconsciousness—that there is no why—that there is always joy, there is always beauty, there is always life and its infinite things when man strives in his soul.

All the characters in the book are concluded according to their development, including the young murderer (who returns from jail repentant, almost saintly, and filled with new courage and ambition and love); none are left hanging in the early parts of the story. The vast number of such characters, acquaintances and friends of Peter, give the book a coverage of broad American types and destinies.

I write with gravity and gleefulness because I do not feel skeptical and clever about these things, and I believe that this is an American feeling. (No Joyce, no Auden, no Kafka has anything to say to a true American.) If much of the writing seems to be over-explained, it's only because I want the majority of readers to understand what goes on in the story, because I believe that the average American can understand anything and everything providing one does not address him in the foreign tongue of European culture-consciousness.

Some Town and City Conclusions (1948)

A form of masochism, (or love of helplessness,) and something that resembles *impetuosity* of a sort seems to make the most conclusive evidence connected with what I have been calling "intellectual decadence." This, which occurs in modern City-Centers in America, along with the crowded, harried, unhealthy, brutal life of the City-Center in general, should be the main subject to be drawn and concluded in the City episode.

The masochism occurs in various forms but springs up from the same patterned depths, the same psychology, the same "character structure," or if not that Reichian term, at least, the same character-dissolution. It concerns a real fall from manliness. I mean this in the most direct sense. And concurrently, in women, it concerns a real fall from womanliness, again in the most direct sense. It renders the man helpless in the real situations of *real* life, that is, a kind of primary life which is arbitrarily sluffed over by the convenient City-forms that can't and never will last. I distinctly remember, in my Bohemian City days, having a horror of life outside the city, as though I were sheltered from it; actually having a horror of the very countryside itself. These feelings were real. A dream I had recently convinced me that this is true: that helplessness is the basis of all neurotic forms in the mind. It is a City Disbelief in the will. City Men like Kafka and Spengler* love nothing better than delineations of horrible destiny which a man is incapable of changing, by which a man is doomed. Since the American idea is a will-idea above all things, the mere fact that helplessness and will-lessness enters into our City-Centers is a dangerous fact indicating a decline of character and just guts in a generation. In these situations, the woman is rendered unwomanlike and *hors de combat*—real barrenness, disbelief in marriage, Lesbianism, Talking-Womanism, general frustrated, impetuous nastiness.

A lot of the magnanimity of our "Liberalism" is connected with masochism. The New York radical who rushes down South to "fight for the Negro" is only impetuously showing he is much better than we are: and at the same time, of course, revealing that he wants to be punished. This is Burroughs, except that he turns to a reversal of values, of Bourgeois values, instead of political reversals. All these radical departures are really *poses* intended to set up an invidious comparison, as malicious as the invidiousness of wealth and position and blood. Since none of these things concern the general run of American mankind (and around the world to boot), I conclude that the people are not mad, it is the intelligentsia which is mad. The people have patience, a sense of humor, sanity, occasional brutality and violence, but in the end, they are fair and square, and strong. Thus it is easy to see how an intelligentsia which bases itself in City-Centers and has the great modern tools of news-dissemination and communication at hand can in the end exert a blighting influence on the children of the people, and ruin future generations. My own motive for saying all these things is partly invidious, partly impetuous,

---

*and Freud in a more insidious sense

mostly serious and concerned with the livelihood of people: if this were not so, I don't think I'd say it, work so hard at saying it in a two-yeared siege (at the height of a sensual feeling for pleasure that most men have in their twenties).

George Martin is dying at the end of the story, but he hangs on to the bitter end with amazing endurance, humor, and courage (which actually happened to my father). And even as he dies, he rues the day he dropped his business in Galloway in a masochistic splurge, and would start all over again if he could. His excessive illness however makes him sensitive and childlike and almost saintly, and he can cry one minute and raise the roof the next, depending on the weather. There is a strong streak of Christian saintliness and Myshkin-idiocy running in men, especially in Martin *père* and son, but the very existence of this streak, which mars their strength, however heightens their sense of real immediate justice in life. This is the proper mixture I think.

PART III

JACK AND LEO KEROUAC

Leo Kerouac served as the prototype for Joe Martin in *The Haunted Life*. This section opens with a series of letters addressed by Leo to Jack and Jack's older sister, Caroline (known affectionately as "Nin"), in which the political volatility of their father is on full display. The content of Leo's letters, addressed to Jack during his brief 1942 stay in Washington, DC, runs the gamut from film and book criticism to the especial vitriol he harbors for Franklin and Eleanor Roosevelt. Writing in the wake of losing his printing business—largely through his own mismanagement and profligate behavior—Leo also expresses a great deal of contempt for Lowell (often referred to as "Stinktown") and Jack's Columbia University football coach Lou Little (referred to on one occasion as a "wop"). Troubling aspects aside, the letter dated "Saturday Eve '42" contains a concluding section titled "AFTERMATH," demonstrating a playfulness with form that his son would have no doubt appreciated.

Moreover, the two typed sketches authored by Leo ("A Sketch of Gerard" and "A Sketch of Nashua and Lowell") suggest that the elder Kerouac may have wielded some early influence over the development of Jack's literary interests and style. The vivid sentimentalism contained within Leo's sketch of Gerard—Jack's older brother who died of rheumatic fever at the age of nine— serves as a portent for Jack's own descriptions of his brother in *Visions of Gerard* (1963). The accompanying sketch of Nashua and Lowell aims in part at criticizing the young Jack's atheistic tendencies, as Leo goes on to openly question whether his son has the resolve to make it through the war years—or through life in general.

Leo—who had been born Joseph Alcide Leon Kerouac in 1889 in Saint-Hubert de-Rivière-du-Loup, Quebec—died from stomach cancer in May 1946. The remaining three documents in this section, penned by Jack, reveal the complexity of the son's relationship to his volatile and bigoted, yet devoted father. The long diary entry from 1945 deals quite specifically with Leo's illness, and declares at one point that sickness has jarred Leo out of his racial obsessions. It also captures Jack within the glow of his heady encounter with New York intellectualism, containing references to Céline, *Partisan Review*, and Lucien Carr's "New Vision." In stating his interest in writing an epic saga of American life, driven by an "urge to understand the whole in one sweep, and to express it in one magnificent work," Jack also admits to feeling alienated by the nation's evolving concerns and institutions—much as he did in the *Town and the City* documents included in the previous section.

"An Example of Non*Spontaneous Deliberated Prose," composed in the jazzed-up style for which Kerouac is most renowned, evokes the author's early memories of Lowell and Leo. Indeed, the nonspontaneous prose referred to in the title is soon revealed to be Leo's, as Jack fondly recalls his father sitting at a typewriter and laboring over an editorial piece for his local tabloid, the *Lowell Spotlight*. Leo's labors stand in contrast to the confident and spontaneous nature of Jack's recollections, featuring a first sentence that runs to 316 words. The final document collected here, a ruminative fragment from 1963, was written in that same spontaneous vein. In it, Kerouac lauds his father for his sincerity, the quality toward which his own work would consistently aspire.

T. F. T.

Letters (1942–1943)

Leo Kerouac

Friday '42
Dear Jack,

Got your address from your mother. She told me about your trip to N.Y.—and I hope you'll be good and give me firsthand news of what goes on.

Washington must be a madhouse and you are very lucky to be at the head of this hysteria. I rather think you'll get invaluable experience which in years to come will be of great value. This country is going through a phase you'll never face again. What a weird future your generation is facing. I thought I had been through an amazing age, but I daresay that your generation will make history as never before in this world.

We made the groundwork, us oldsters, with our inventive and generally energetic years, and now for the jackpot! "Hold her boys, she's going to be a whopper!" Oil. You've got a whale of a gusher. And I hope the operators know how to get her in hand. She's raining now and whew! Will they ever cap and control it?

Dig in Jack! Get it all. Keep away from Lowell. Go and see things. Use your head and your heart. Remember your old folks. Your mom, she loves you, and Caroline and I will stand by and that's all we can do.

Don't get false ideas. Don't think for instance that I've given you up. You're a strange boy, but you're still my very dear hustling, quizzling little kid with your old fringed hat, a brown healthy tan, a craving for ice cream, and your mom's good cooking.

What did you do about Joe Doakes?* How did he finally pan out? You know, you have a real idea there. Sleep on it. And so after a while, say in about six months, put your teeth in it and give it all you got, and something will come of it, believe me.

You probably want some news about me. Jack, I've got the little job I've always dreamed about. Good bosses. Swell guys to work with—(I hope you'll come and see me sometime. I'll introduce you to my new gang)—and I'm beginning to call my soul my own again. Meriden is a small town. 2 movies, but I go to Hartford almost every week and have a show and dinner, and generally pass the time of day fairly well.

It's lonesome of course, but I really don't mind it. Lowell is on the boom they tell me. Celebrating because they're going to make things to kill the youth of the world. Isn't that Lowell for you. God, what a rat hole. Thank God I have not had to keep making death dealing things and I hope that I may never have to do that. I make a small pay, but it's all green and is not stained red with the blood of the vast army of the world's underprivileged.

My health is good, eat regularly, except this week. (Bet a plug) you know, so missed a few breakfasts. Not having your ability to rhapsodize in words, I could eat a big meal just now—and it wouldn't even make a dent in my middle. I spend $18 regularly, make or break, and that's that.

---

* *Joe Doakes* is period slang for the average man, since replaced by *Joe Blow.* It is unclear whom Leo is referring to in this case.

Be *practical* Jack. Put yourself on a budget, send money home every week if you go to work, by special delivery and *money order*—it's the best way to handle that. Your mom tells [me] you're going to make good money, so don't waste it, and we will find it handy later for the completion of your education.

If you're drafted take it with good grace. Don't be a slacker and put yourself behind the 8-ball. Be courageous, and trust to luck, they don't all get it!—and the things you'll see and run across will make a better and greater man of you. You must resolve that you are grown up and assume the responsibilities of your new estate.

That isn't preaching, Jack, only a word to encourage you I hope, for the trying times ahead of you. As for us, we must realize what it all means, our only son, facing the horrors and uncertainties of what is to come. It is a heavy cross to bear, and more so for us than you can imagine.

I don't know whether all I've said so far means anything to you, for I've given up trying to interest you some years ago. I realize the gulf between the old gang and the new generation. There are so many things I cannot understand about you but I have faith that time and experience will bring us around to a better understanding, and you on the verge of upheavals which will either make or break you.

So I'll close now and hope I may see you sometime this summer, maybe in N.Y. some Sunday. They run excursions every week and we might meet if you decide to work in Washington.

Give my love to Old Roosie, and dear! dear! Eleanoah!—the sweet thing! Bet you get a whiff when she's in town.*

---

* These are derogatory references to Franklin and Eleanor Roosevelt.

Be brave, be gay, be a regular guy—always! That's the way to live. Don't repent! Don't forget your Dad, your Mother, your sister—all A-1 rooters.

The old weasel—
POP

Saturday Eve, '42

Dog my cat, so I whelped a Gigolo—that's what Roosie does to everyone in America, makes 'em into what they ain't meant to be—or ever dreamed they were. Ask Charlie Lindbergh and others who tried to do some straight thinking. Anyway, don't let the Washington merry-go-round make you permanently dizzy.

Are you saving money kid? It's mighty handy sometimes. Have you sent some home—and did you remember your mom on Mother's Day, or did a blonde make you forget her?

Your letter was most welcome and it pleased me immensely. I hope you'll find time to write as often as you can. I didn't get it [about] Brooklyn! I haven't much to say because I'm afraid if I say things you'll think I am trying to preach. If you have too many skirts, send me one willya! Ain't there a cast-off redhead that ain't too fussy? Woo-woo.

Oh, seriously Jack, am going home over Memorial Day, it being on Saturday it will give me a couple of days, and so I am going to visit my home. Ain't dat sumtin'. Too bad you'll be so very far away, we could have a little reunion (Could it be arranged?).

You tell me you take naps on your job. Gosh, I hope you should try to keep this job. The money you can make would probably mean a lot to you next Fall.

I am rambling a lot. My mind is not on writing and so just consider this note a little greeting and my fervent wish for your welfare through these trying times—keep your head. Think clean, act clean, don't let your life become sordid.

—*POP*

(AFTERMATH—or sumpin)

Gosh, I don't know Jack. I got to tell you about some of the good things I ran across the past few weeks.

Read Upton Sinclair's latest book *Dragon's Teeth*, mighty clear story of what the shooting is all about. I don't know whether you'd like it—but it is a very clear picture of the rise of Adolph Schicklgruber—and shows just how the power of politics operates in the hands of scatterbrains!*

And for a picture, 4 bells to "Butch Minds the Baby," Damon Runyon's story. A little gem, with real laughs, an adorable baby, and human! I liked it so much I actually squirmed in my seat. And a great cast, too, wait till you see the guy with the "specs" who was nearly blind from drinking prohibition booze. It's New Yorkers— and how! Ronnie Reagan and the curvaceous Annie Sheridan do a pretty fine job in "King's Row" also. And Rooney's latest. "Doc" [?] Kildare. The new glam in Kildare looks like a Jew to me. Too bad they didn't give a real kid the part, it's a honey.

Am reading translations of Guy de Maupassant. What a dart! I sometimes wonder if guys like him are great writers or just plain, common double-action jerks. They sure sound like 'em in spots—but they can tell good stories, and how they love the [?]. I can imagine how they would read in French!

---

* The reference here is to Adolf Hitler and is based on what was then a popular (but fallacious) belief that Hitler originally bore the surname of his paternal grandmother, Maria Anna Schicklgruber.

fast. So that's strike one for Willkie. He'll step in later and reap the spoils from the gang that is already in, strip 'em of their dough [?] a great war job and be the Lincoln of his day, and I wouldn't be surprised if he has to do it [?] way he'll be glad to boss the job. He is a good boss you know.

His record, man to man, is so far ahead of Roosey in actual achievement as day to night. Roosie was born in the velvet and won't part with his trimming unless they take it away from him. Willkie got his the hard way and hasn't much, has rubbed elbows with the working man and he knows his answers. Does that make sense to you? If Willkie sees the light he can go places. That's my reaction.

You ask me to write up the stooges of old Stinktown. I'd get writer's cramp and there's so much of it. I'd need a typewriter—and I haven't got one, along with a lot of other things I haven't got. After all, it would only add up to a cross-section of small-time punks and that has been done to death.

So you're out of football at Columbia. How it bears out. My observations weren't any too far wrong. "A fart by any other name" would stink as much. You're like your old dad—bet your bundle on the wrong stag that time—but other days, other places—it's not too late. You should try it with the Navals should you be lucky enough to get in eventually. I wish the day would come when you could show Old Shit-Face that you're a better man than he is. Wops!*

---

* The reference here is to Jack's football coach at Columbia, Lou Little, whose birth name was Luigi Piccolo. Leo's accompanying reference to the "Navals" pertains to the US Naval Academy, whose football team was a regular opponent of Columbia at the time.

I read through one of these Saroyan books, 25 cent paper covered. I still have it. Well, my candid opinion is that he is an exalted gutter-snipe. He reminds me much of [?] in his serious moments. They both seem to be amazed at the ease with which they
make good. There's nothing solid or substantial to any of them.
They're both good observing reporters, that's all. Since the world
is full of [?]—we all know it and the European Species falls back
on Old Women's tales from the Old Countries and they wallow
in it [?] their own personalities, and there you have your Saroyan.
A cockroach on the loose. Observing the intricacies of the other vermin that crossed their path. They talk about irresponsibil-
ities of life because they are that way themselves, and so are the
source[s] of these ideas.

True culture and real worth lies in a different direction I believe. I still stick with the French when it comes to feelings and
a keener understanding of life. Their books, their movies show
a complete superiority over the American products which in my
estimation, in our modern world, are among the best. We must
not forget our Swedish, Norwegian, English and other toilers
who are right up front in the parade. Germany has lost its mo-
mentum under Hitler and the last war's impact. What the future
holds will be determined by the results of this war we are now
thrashing out.

Now that I've tried to say a few things, I suppose you'll laugh
at my puny efforts at analyzing things.

Sunday, March 24, 1945
Dear Caroline,

Here I am with a sheet stuck in the typewriter, and trying to think of what I should say. I know you want news about us, what we're doing, thinking, how things are. Well, your mother covers that pretty well in her many letters to you, and so I'm stuck with the morale end of it. My own morale is not at high pitch as you know.

We see many things here in a large city, and I doubt if there is a more corrupt or ridiculous city in the world than New York. It simply cannot be summed up in a few paragraphs. It would take a book and a big one to explain its people, politics, depravity, and the occasional good things there are in it.

And I can't see that it would be very interesting to most people. It is not a part of America, and maybe on the other hand, it expresses America and its prevalent hypocrisies better than anything else can. THANK God that we have our small apartment away from the center of the city where it seems intolerable to have to live.

We haven't heard from Paul lately, so I suppose no news is good news.* How about you? Hope that you are well and as happy as circumstances permit? Jack lives with us, with a skip now and then. He has written a book which he hopes they will publish. But that's as far as it got so far. A publisher has it now for two weeks, and was supposed to let him know this weekend. He went away last Friday night and now, Sunday afternoon, he hasn't shown up. He had a few dollars he earned with small jobs, and went on one of his intellectual? binges, I suppose.

---

* Paul Blake, Caroline's husband.

The story deals with the screwy stuff that happens every day in New York, and it isn't all nice stuff by any means. It tells the story of some European whackie who comes here at a tender age, and finally lands in the jug after a murder he commits, because he is being pursued by another man??? Just imagine that!!!

As for myself, I work anytime I feel like it. Was subbing at a newspaper this week, and got $71.25 for my week's pay, so you see it could be worse. They kept me on for two other days, with a prospect of fairly steady subbing work. It's easy work, and I'm going to do this a while, as I have some $65 vacation money coming, and I'm anxious to lay my hands on this money. The Union has it, they keep it and pay off once a year after April 1st.

I'll probably stick around visiting museums, zoos, etc., and buy myself some clothes if I can find them. I really need new clothes. I feel like a bum as usual, with my broken teeth and wrinkled rage.

Your mother seems well, complains of being tired, and I guess she is, it's a question who is the more tired, her or I. Jack sleeps all day anyway, so that makes it even. Hope you are the same, like Uncle Ezra would say, by gum. Yer lovin' father

THE WEAZEL

A Sketch of Gerard (1942)

Leo Kerouac

A very tired limping man turns in the street leading home. He has just been through a searing siege of sickness which nearly finishes him, but life and its obligation. His little Gerard, chubby Jack, jolly little Caroline, and a distracted nearly-driven crazy mother finally pulled him through. He just wouldn't die, so he lived, and miserably for months and months.

And now a new sorrow enters his life. Ridden with debt, working under unbearable conditions, caused by that life-sapping sickness, his beloved little boy, his little favorite, his little Gerard, his first born was ailing—and it began to dawn that a leaking valve of the heart was the cause and he was so sweet, ah, my dear God, so sweet. And so pitiful, what father's heart could ever bear to look!

And as he turns towards home, Gerard is eagerly waiting for his daddy, he really loved his dad, Oh I knew it, felt it. Sitting on the arm of my chair at night, telling him evasive little things to make him give out his sad little smile, and he'd kiss me on the cheek, shy, pecking little things that hurt, hurt, hurt, Oh, God.

That night Gerard is waiting eagerly, but my slow steps are not fast enough for his love. He must run out to me, meet me, and I pick him up, saying, "Poor little sonny, why did you run, you know you shouldn't." "But I wanted to meet you daddy" and I pressed him so tenderly to me, with eyes honestly full of tears. I didn't care what neighbors saw. Gerard was my ALL, my sweet. Loving little animals, loving life! And he had such a short, short time to live it.

And as I press him to my heart, and limp along with him, holding him dearly, lovingly, his little heart is beating against mine, and that beating, ah, dear God, that beating—Life ebbing away. And I knew it, and couldn't bear it, but clung to him with tears in my eyes and heart. "Don't you feel my heart beating, Pop?" he asks. "Feel, see how hard it beats." "Yes," I answer, "yes, Gerard, God gave you too big a heart, and that's why it beats so hard. It's too big for your body, and that isn't good," I told him. And he smiled his sad smile, as he knew that angels were waiting for him, for he was too good for this earth.

And so it came to pass. One night I could not stand it any longer. I had business, so instead of staying home, I got away from the pain for a moment, and Gerard asked his mother why I was always going away. Why? And that night, the angels came, and left me nothing but the sweet, tender memory of the really only one that ever mattered in my life. I cried like a child for weeks, and wore a black necktie for over a year, and by and by the memory became hallowed, but even as I write this I barely can see the typewriter keys—it is as vivid as the night of June 5th, the night the angels claimed my—Gerard.

A Sketch of Nashua and Lowell (1942)

Leo Kerouac

This is the narration of a little episode of some forty-five years ago. Yes, it's a long, long time ago.

A little boy is sitting dejectedly, tired, hot, on the curbstone of a street in Nashua. But look—there's something strange too. He has one perfect leg, but the other is a useless thing, barely as large as a grown man's forefinger, every bone traced by its skin covering. It's a leg that has stopped growing. A pitiful sight! The little fellow is moodily spanning the scene of going and coming people, wagons, with the dust of horses' hoofs covering his sweaty little feet. He is not far from home, but for him it seems thousands of miles away. You see, the poor kid can't walk very well, and every step is misery. He has a rickety little crutch to help him along, but that's hardly the thing he needs to carry his puny weight home. A cord was twined around running from his useless leg to his shoulder, thereby saving it from actual contact with the weight of his body as he hopped along on one foot and his crutch.

A kind-hearted woman stops and bends over. "Are you far away from home, little boy?" she asked with moist eyes. "No, just around the corner at the end of the street," answered the child. Four years old, hardly lisping his answers. "Won't you let me carry you home, sonny?" "No," answers the boy quickly, so he struggles up with the aid of his crutch, and lopes off, finally reaching home where his mother tenderly picks him up, and kisses his worried little face into smiles.

We lived at the end of a street, and one night, a tall, kindly looking man with flowing beard, knocks at the door, and asks for a night's lodging. He seems so good and kind, that both father and mother quickly accede to his demands. And after the evening meal, in the old fashioned parlor, he speaks of the little boy with the useless leg. After a series of questions, he picks up the lad and takes his foot in hand, and begins to bend and twist the useless thing, asking every second if this or that more hurts. The little lad answers and "ouches" a few times. But somehow from that moment things began to happen to that leg, and it began to grow and came in time to bear up to 250 pounds of flesh in all kinds of conditions. The boy never became a star athlete because of that leg, but was one of the best swimmers the YMCA ever produced locally, and he could twist and bend his body with wonderful agility.

A strange story, a true one, and one that never has been explained. What fate sent that man to our house. Who was he? I am now 53 years old, weigh 240 and am hale and hearty and that leg still serves very well, outside of a few twinges occasionally, when it has to stand too long on a hard floor. Explain that one, my fine atheist. Yes, I still believe in a short prayer every night—and in times of stress.

AND HERE's another laugh! Was in Lowell in the '11s. We were being examined, a physical examination at the YMCA. The doctor had me strip, and "Whew," he exclaimed, "What a man! You are one of the finest specimens of young manhood I have ever had the pleasure to examine," he told me. And I laughed and said "Baloney," Where did he get that stuff! But one leg was much smaller than its mate. It never bothered me in them days, I was so radiantly alive and full of things to do, and—doing them. And now—well, you know what has become of all this. And I am afraid that life will beat you too Jack—and you think I'm jealous when I'm only skeptical. I'VE been through it—but you have to FACE it, and it's not a picnic, now more than ever!

There's the thought. Have we given you enough FIGHT to go through it? We gave you the body, you have the brains, have YOU got the fight? There it is in a nutshell!

You're always saying: Why don't you write.

Maybe I'm in the mood. Was sittin' by the radio and strains of "I Love You Truly" just set my mind workin'—on a little episode in the good years so far back now. The scene is laid in a Montreal nightclub. Or was it a nightclub strictly speaking? Surely there were few people there that night, as I remember it. We were all sitting together around one long table.

It was a big family gathering of your mother's folks. Doc, Carmen, Alice, your cousin Irene, and a raft of smaller cousins, their wives, and we were having a real good time, with Gilles Champeau as a self appointed master of behind-the-scenes cere-monies. Wine and beer, and good liquor flowed fast and frequent, everybody was in high spirits.

The real master of ceremonies was a youngster, a fine type of young Canadian, French speaking who has a beautiful sing-ing voice, and your mother finally got him to sing "I Love You Truly"—and truly he sang it with such feeling and so beautifully did he render the enchanting old song, that every time I hear it, it brings back the pain and sweetness of these happy-go-lucky days—you know Jack, my Plymouth car, and the barging around we used to do with it.

These days are far, far behind. They'll never be back I know that, but would you ask me that I had it differently, and I'd say "No, no." The joy of sitting and basking in [a] friendly, enlivened family reunion, everybody smiling laughing, a little bit under the weather, but all supremely palpitating—full of the goodness of life, a moment to be cherished, never to be forgotten. Kin-ties that never, never can be equaled. All of them with their feebleness, their glory, their heart-wracking, pitiful small lives magically transformed for a few hours, into an hour of real communion, of real friendship, of real understanding. All their virtues shining, all their feeble vague small sins forgotten for one night, one wholesome moment, when everything seems enchanted, happy, gay—living and content.

"I Love You Truly," your mother's selection. A lonesome heart reaching out for understanding, for forgiveness perhaps. I never knew. Living a moment in the sweet rendition of a perfect song. But your mother was lonesome—I had been all my life, have been. No fault of ours, just things that are stranger than fiction. I always knew and understood her better than she did herself. She made much of this unknown young man, and he was a fine, pleasant young fellow, an understanding, kind-hearted chap, humoring her whim and her motherly advances with a frank grin, a twinkle in his eye, and oh so wise. I admired this young fellow greatly. I couldn't help it. He seemed to know things—and we always cotton up to guys who know.

Why do I write this? It's only a whim. I'm sorry for many things that have gone, and not at all at fault I think. It was just Old Devil Life having his little fun, laughing at us—he always did.

We tried—and the cards were stacked as they are generally. But "I Love You Truly"—just what is love? Is it the passion of a minute, or the understanding that years thrust upon us? I do not know. And thank God, or the fates, that your mother has someone to-day, that "life without you" would mean a barren, mean life.

So you see Jack, we are all born for a purpose. Yours is des-tined—Love her, cherish her beyond all things, for from her you will get all that is good and sweet in life, years will make you real-ize this. All other loves in your life will seem drab in comparison, when the years have rolled by band memories only will remain. "I Love You Truly" in Montreal, on a summer night, with the family. Is this trash—maybe, I don't know, but there's a thought in it, carry on where I've failed, make life full and rich for her, and then only can I be or feel vindicated.

Diary Entry (1945)

JACK KEROUAC

(Some very convincing words I read today by Julian Green . . . admittedly, I am under the sway of such men. He said one should keep a perpetual diary. Now that I think of it, if I had kept a diary of the events of the summer of 1944 I should now have material for a fine book . . . love, murder, diabolical conversations, all. Now it's too late of course to catch such full-blown living tragedies as they drop from the branch, it's too late to catch *that* one. I begin this diary in the faith and certitude that other things equally dramatic will happen to me, one time or another. And Green says that what you put down in your diary, however dull, is always of extreme, almost excruciating interest later on. Yes, I see that . . . a few lines of conversation, a few scenes from the past: these I would eat hungrily. So I begin.)

August 21

TODAY I WAS AROUSED at ten o'clock from a deep sleep (sleeping off an intoxication with Céline's "Journey to the End of the Night"!) . . . it was the Red Cross calling. My sister, in an Army camp in Indiana, was arranging to come home on the strength of father's imminent operation for tumor at the Brooklyn hospital.

The Red Cross wanted my father's doctor's name and phone number. My sister's losing no time. The war is over, she wants to come home, and wait for her husband, Paul, who is at present in Okinawa. Father's illness presents her with a splendid opportunity. After the call, I took a cold shower and busied myself with a trip to Columbia University, where I must get transcripts of my Columbia marks sent on their way to the University of California. Trouble, however . . . with the Registrar there, who wants the $178 I owe the place. I went and surreptitiously arranged things with an employee. It may come off, *qui sais?* After that, I went to the Columbia libraries, several of them, and read. Julian Green; on the life of James Joyce; read *Kenyon Review, Partisan Review* . . . all the dull intellectualism getting nowhere at all, a chiaroscuro of chaos. I was mad to find out more about Louis-Ferdinand Céline, but no one seems to bother about him. He is an alien, that madman. I think there are thousands of geniuses like him in Europe, one on every street corner, who never bother to write. The same cannot be said of America, I think, or perhaps I'm wrong. Céline has driven me into a new mad flight of thought . . . perhaps he has changed my life, as Thomas Wolfe did. I'm certain he has changed my life, at this minute. No Spengler, no Rilke, no Yeats, not even a Rimbaud has moved me quite as much, from top to bottom as it were.

I was planning to stay in town and see either Gilmore or Seymour, and then I decided to go and see my father after all (to prove that I was aloof from the tragedy of my own life, and able to transcend it and remain intact, in mind, and not in nature, for my writing). I went to the hospital. He was sitting on the verandah with mother. He is facing a very serious operation . . . he is of course, gloomy and a bit frightened. They are going to extract a tumor from him. We are all rotten inside, that's what we are. Life is by nature rotten. All of nature is rotten. Conversely, all bacilli are rotten too, because they rot themselves when they cannot feed on rottable flesh . . . something to that effect. It was a great scene. I sat watching my father. His hair was awry, over a bald exposed dome, like a corpse I'd once seen in the Bellevue morgue. We talked. My father is learning a lot in the hospital; all the racial nonsense is gone, he sees all men how they are, one by one . . . and all women, of course. A friendly attendant chatted with us, and explained the law of nature. It was amusing and terrifying. I realized then that I was all *mind*—that I was hardly aware of my own rotten body, ever. "A high meeting of nature and mind," that's man. My mother and I left after a while. I wanted to show my father that I felt terrible, by touching his hand as I left him. But I didn't. Constraint. Constraint in the face of death. I only went through the normal channels of feeling such as kissing him. A touch of the hand, at parting, means much more. We all walk around, losing each other, thinking about it, getting lost ourselves, all vague, and then when the end comes, we are surprised and all tragic. Poo! We are all sealed in our own little melancholy atmospheres, like planets, and revolving around the sun, our common but distant desire. I shall never forget that scene on the verandah. It was because there was the knowledge that my father might die, but of course I don't believe that he will at all. But the knowledge was there. A cool wind came across the trees in the street. There was a dusky calm. My father's wispy hair moved in the wind. I watched my mother, and kept my thoughts to myself; and then I watched my father. We were all involved in a deep realization of what life really is like. It's gradually losing your salt, is life. Tomorrow my father will lose so much more of his salt. As Gide puts it, where can he get back that salt again?

The attendant finished off the whole picture, telling how fish eats fish, and how animals ignore their infirm. You start a baby, presumably new and full of salt, and then you grow and gradually lose it all . . . not forgetting the fact that a baby is of course itself a little rotten piece of humanity. A dead baby stinks as much as a dead old man. The attendant gave off these impressions. He himself is bulging with a hernia, he is white and yellow with cirrhosis of the liver, and may even himself have a tumor or cancer. He handles the dead ones in the hospital. One man died while my father was being washed by this attendant, right in the next bed. The man jumped up and fell back sideways, bumping his head on the wall, and was dead. Someone yelled at the attendant, "He needs you!" The attendant left my father there and went to the dead man. Later he took him down to the refrigerated morgue in the cellar. My father says you get a little cooling before hell, in this day of marvels. Enough.

My mother and I came home. I went to bed, too tired to write anymore. (I'm composing a novel.) Things are as they are . . . and Job says "Things too wonderful for me." *Peut-entre, mon petit.* I myself mistrust the lyric now more than ever.

August 22

AFTER I HAD DISPATCHED a little matter in the city concerning money-earning, I came home to learn from mother and sister . . . the very wretched worst about my father. He is dying of cancer of the spleen. Tonight, in the hospital, while I lie sleepless for him, for everything, for myself, here—does he not also lie sleepless? What is he thinking? I see him going down the street past that last streetlamp there; into the darkness . . . Are there fields there for him? He loves fields, goddammit. We sat around the house, my sister and mother and I, discussing the problem of money . . . hospitalization, all that. I had an urge to disappear, never to come back to sickness and death and the suffocation of my own life and blood. I took a three mile walk . . . the murderous summer, the murderous moon, the fratricidal madness in me, the patricidal insanity worst of all . . . Yes, he has lost his salt, all of it soon. MY FATHER IS DYING AND I CANNOT FIND THE LANGUAGE, and that is what is most damnable: Goodbye, sweet thoughts. How can I ever again face myself? Who on earth am I? How is it that he is my father, and that I am his son . . . Once when he was younger, he almost died: the doctor had pulled the sheet over his face: that frightened him! In a moment he was up, sitting in a chair. He should never, never have met my mother. Or had he died then, I should have become something other than what I am now, mooning in the night, by the full brooding moon of murderous August.

Alas, I tried to write tonight. I could not find the language. Already, Ferdinand Céline is slipping from me, and I myself am slipping back to myself, to myself which is not enough. But one must be oneself! . . . I was annoyed, thinking of Julian Green, and how he had written "The Closed Garden" . . . calmly, in the country, imagining the woman. Were his gifts abided before he received them? Did he not suffer? . . . and I thought of all the others, the immeasurable suffering everywhere. Pounded pillows! One is worsened each passing day . . . it is truly a stairway down to knowledge, a "journey down into the night." I said to myself, my father dies but I shall not die with him. I said that because I thought I had artistry. Then I didn't have it, all of a sudden, I've never had it.

Artistry!—no mere word any more, no metaphysical, methodological concept. It's something now purely a personal matter. To hell with the rest of the world, and artistic theories, and art. Artistry is my life: it's sunk down to that, to me alone, alone and dark me, and without it I won't live . . . not for a jot. It's down to this now: I am only interested in life and people insofar as it enters my mind to become art. Otherwise, I am aloof, disinterested, bored, and dying too. This is my "one superb idea." To die with someday. And it hasn't come! Meanwhile, *he* dies! What shall I say to him? He who will not die, dies . . . This is my entry for the day.

Une autre chause: my sister came home; he saw her, coming out of ether for a while, and kissed her hand. He was laughing, too, like Leon Robinson. Laughing! waving his hand at them out of the netherworld he was in, just before falling back into it, waving at them. I wasn't there . . . I couldn't have borne it, quickly like that to know. Tomorrow I go there to see him. He doesn't know. Of course, he must never see this diary. I must hide it. I may be killing him writing all this, as he forages through my papers all the time. He won't see this, however, if he ever comes home at all.

I lie at night staring at his empty bed nearby. He who snored so ponderously. Well, that is life and death. We all know it, yet none of us *realize* it. Even he, perhaps, does not realize it . . . throwing himself back to life in confusion. Yet I know he knows! and realizes! My father is a great man. That is borne by facts which I shall later bring out.

I am betraying my life, all that concerns my life, if I cannot find the language. That's what it's down to: something personal like that, with all the theories gone forever. I am betraying my life, my father, if I do not find the language.

August 23

BUT OF COURSE THERE WERE DISCREPANCIES in my mother's gloomy prognostications. I went to the hospital myself, today with sister, and spoke to the doctor. He's not sure it's cancer . . . Just an oversized spleen, too big, too, to take out . . . Father's tremendous anger with folly and injustice! It's the spleen, you see! He will be home in ten days: we will see what happens. In the meantime we are all relieved. And there is an understanding now between my father and I that bids fair to be of an epic-heroic quality, yes! Never was Oedipus so reconciled with his father! . . . and on such grounds! I can resume my art without having to force my own life behind it, in the cruel lifeless fashion that is necessary in such matters. Practically speaking, I can go to college and have enough to eat. On to the nebulous future, then, in good cheer.

September 3

My father is quite well now . . . it was all a mix-up. Of course he'll never be his old self again, but *c'est la vie* . . .

Today, Labor Day, a clear sunny day with the tender blue char in the sky hinting of October, I felt a resurgence of the old feeling, the old Faustian urge to understand the whole in one sweep, and to express it in one magnificent work—mainly, America and American life. Bunting, flying leaves, families drinking beer in their own backyards, cars filling the highways (the war being over officially now), children tanned and ready for school, the smell of roasts coming from the cottages on the leafy streets, the whole rich American life in one panorama. I had the feeling that I was alien to all this, as I walked around . . . that all this could never be mine to have, only mine to express. I felt like an exile. I told this to my mother, saying that perhaps we were too French to be American, with a little too much of the bleak severe Breton in our lives and not enough emphasis on its fire and Celtic passion . . . Everyone in America today, Sept. 3, 1945, is out rushing around in a car, on the highways, at beaches, celebrating Labor Day, the end of the war, celebrating life, anything . . . just so long as they can celebrate. All of this, the cottages with laughter and good food and wine, the cars on the highways, the radios blaring, the flags and bunting—all of this, not for my likes, never. It's strange, since I'm aware that I understand all this far more completely than the people who do have the American richness in them . . . Perhaps I don't want it, that may be so. Other things I do want. I was reminded today of a conversation in Greenwich Village last summer: Mimi West had asked me what I was looking for, in my writing that is, and I had told her, "A new method." At this point, Lucien Carr had put in: "A new method! . . . and a new vision." Well, he was wrong; the vision I do have, it's the method I want . . . the vision cannot be expressed without the method. The vision is all there, it was painfully there for me to comprehend all day today, as I walked around . . . Someday I'll express it. I've no doubt that I will.

Progress on the Phillip Tourian novel, the personal version of it sans collaboration, is good; 25,000 words in the past week. Céline has opened a gap in me, not the whole gap, but enough to release as much as there is allowed.

An Example of Non*Spontaneous Deliberated Prose (October 11, 1954)

JACK KEROUAC

ONE PURE AFTERNOON in that prime of time which is Indian Summer in the sad northern earth, in America hard heard echoed in the trumpet's slow blues as chewed thoughtfully from the lips of dejected jazz musicians with rings under their eyes philosophizing upon things of the day in the depths of the club night, olden & golden light falling thru fire escape & registering bars shadowy in alley of oldtime tar, 1922, the sky singed a burnt hazel orange as if the summer worn edges of the blue, & from the streets of towns & cities there rises that sleepy good shimmer of sun heated manures & oils and befumed activities of the daily workaday dream, Man you see there selfbelievingly & heartbreakingly walking forth with the perfect accommodation of some liquid ghost in a magical action inside mind or imprinted upon the bliss screen of essential Pity in some central Void Night for naught, so that in the instant of death you can imagine someone must have thought "Oh all things were but ignorant forms of pity!," a young printer who was my father Leo Kerouac of Lowell Mass. sat at his rolltop desk his curly black head caught in dust motes snowing in their shaft of afternoon, his face stormy with frowns of Breton dark, ceremonious in a vest & shirtsleeves rolled

187

back showing thick earnest arms, body propped forward eagerly at the iron glooms of an old black typewriter with the arch of his back where the glistening vest drew out the frowsed shirt belying his excitement, thinking, in the honesties of his French Canadian heart "To write this old column right, how things were 25 years ago in Lowell why then, by gosh, how'm I gonna make the folks read it to sound like it was real *then* like things are real *now*, unless I sneak in a little oldtime regrets." With both forefingers he plapped on the keys, popeyed to compose, time of the essence for his Friday night edition of the 8-page theatrical tabloid the Spot Light, 2¢ a copy but distributed free on Friday nights to patrons of Lowell movie theaters elbowing out at midnight to streets so sad you'd think the fresh rose of 8 o'clock curtain lay there tired and worn and nowgrit, and it came out on the page as follow: "25 YEARS AGO In the old days one of the biggest of the theatrical hits ever scored here—"

Reflection on Leo (1963)

JACK KEROUAC

I thank God that, in bringing me to birth in this world which is so sorrowful that the bones of delicate ladies are laid to dust, dust indeed, I mean dirt, dirty old muddy old dirt all that sweetness of face and hands and ladylike arrangements all gone to worms who come a-eyein' em even before the last Te Deum is done in the chapel or the church, in this world so really paradoxically unbearable when you come to think of it, where little infants die without a blot on their brows, God, in giving me birth in this mess of messes called life, did at least let me issue from the loins of my father Leo Alcide Kerouac who was the only honest man I ever knew and the only completely honest expresser of what he thought about the world and the people in it.

Not that there aren't other honest men but I haven't met them yet, except one or two, who nevertheless have some kind of false optimism to cover up the shame of their knowing that they have so much, have tricks borrowed from the philosophies of others, or bury themselves in aimless works, devices, explanations like eager condemned men on the witness stand, name it. But my father sat stunned and naked under these stars and breathed nothing but despair and knew it and said so, and told me so.

The last months of his life on his deathbed he told me things in the middle of the night that would make your hair stand on end.

I've written elsewhere about his early days, his birth in St. Hubert Quebec (not the St. Hubert near Montreal but the one up north near the Gaspe Peninsula, near a town called Rivière du Loup which was said to belong to the Kerouacs before the English entrepreneurs of 1770 or thereabouts took it away by legal shenanigans). I've written about his early hale days as insurance man, printer, happy-go-lucky strawhatted goodtime family man of Lowell Mass. and even got to the later days when, after losing his printing business because of gambling debts (horses and cards), he fell on evil days wandering around dismal little New England towns as part time linotypist going wherever the union sent him. It was during this time that beastly bastardly nature was making me, his son, hit a tremendous halcyon glowing youthful stride . . . the thought of it makes me ashamed. But so now he was transferring the hopes of his own youth onto me.

I was a good athlete and a good scholar and I was headed for college in New York with a halo round my hair and big thick legs in wool socks.

Acknowledgments

My deepest gratitude is reserved for John Sampas, literary executor of the Kerouac estate. John's comprehensive knowledge of Kerouac's archive continually astounds me, and this book would not have been possible without his insightful, generous, and intrepid spirit. I have taken great joy from our conversations regarding these materials (and a wide range of other topics), many of which have taken place in the very home in which the youthful Sebastian and Jack conspired upon their literary ambitions. I hope that John will be pleased by this book, as it owes much to his enthusiasm and sagacity.

Justine DeFeo logged a great number of hours as my research and editorial assistant on this project, though her eagerness and commitment to detail never dimmed. Her rapt fascination with all things Kerouac and her exhilaration in the face of new ideas made Justine a true pleasure to be around. I am extremely proud of the work that she did on this volume and I hope that she learned as much as I did along the way.

Several years ago, my longtime friend Bob Comeau drew me into his knowledgeable fascination with the life and music of Dmitri Shostakovich. The closing pages of my introduction would have been unthinkable without his influence.

This book also owes a tremendous debt to several of my colleagues at the University of Massachusetts Lowell, each of whom contributed their particular wisdom and intelligence to the thoughts collected here. At an early stage, Andre Dubus III looked over the archival materials I had assembled, then aided me in thinking about how they might be arranged. His insights and questions were instrumental to the structure of this volume. Mike Millner and I have worked together on numerous Kerouac-related projects since I arrived at UML in 2011, and I am continually inspired by the degree of fervor, thoughtfulness, and rigor animating his teaching, scholarship, and public humanities efforts. Mike's ideas and sense of intellectual commitment have been invigorating and influential. The various insights of Anthony Szczesiul, Keith Mitchell, Jonathan Silverman, and Chad Montrie have also influenced my writing in this volume. I hope that each of them recognizes his distinctive contributions.

Robert Guinsler of Sterling Lord Literistic provided tremendous help and support at every stage of this endeavor, as did the editorial team at Da Capo—especially Ben Schafer, Carolyn Sobczak, and John Searcy.

Melissa Hudasko—my darling Mishka—has lived with this project across the entire arc of its development. She remains my first and final reader, my fellow traveler through a world of ideas and experience uniquely our own. The range of Melissa's curiosities and abilities continues to astound and humble me, and I am incredibly grateful to share this life (and all of its involving mysteries) with her.

T. F. T.

TODD F. TIETCHEN is an Assistant Professor of English at the University of Massachusetts at Lowell, where he teaches courses in Beat writing and contemporary American literature. He is the author of *The Cubalogues: Beat Writers in Revolutionary Havana*, along with numerous articles on American art, literature, and intellectual history.